MISTLETOE, MUTTS, AND MURDER

a Samantha Davies mystery

S.A. Kazlo

*To Ann Marie (Mimi) and Margaret Laurine for letting
me borrow their lovely names.*

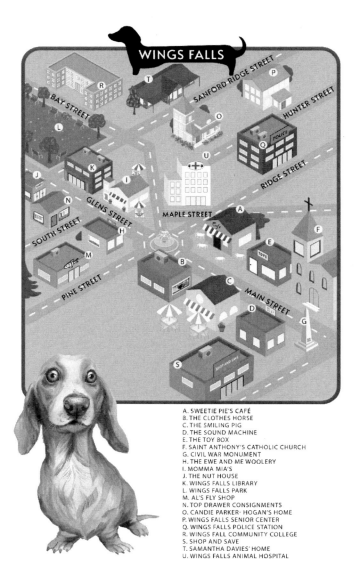

WINGS FALLS

A. SWEETIE PIE'S CAFÉ
B. THE CLOTHES HORSE
C. THE SMILING PIG
D. THE SOUND MACHINE
E. THE TOY BOX
F. SAINT ANTHONY'S CATHOLIC CHURCH
G. CIVIL WAR MONUMENT
H. THE EWE AND ME WOOLERY
I. MOMMA MIA'S
J. THE NUT HOUSE
K. WINGS FALLS LIBRARY
L. WINGS FALLS PARK
M. AL'S FLY SHOP
N. TOP DRAWER CONSIGNMENTS
O. CANDIE PARKER- HOGAN'S HOME
P. WINGS FALLS SENIOR CENTER
Q. WINGS FALLS POLICE STATION
R. WINGS FALL COMMUNITY COLLEGE
S. SHOP AND SAVE
T. SAMANTHA DAVIES' HOME
U. WINGS FALLS ANIMAL HOSPITAL

Acknowledgements

A huge thank you to my Thursday night GFWG. Without you this wouldn't happen. You helped me bring to life, Sam, Porkchop, and all the other characters who people Wings Falls.

A big thank you to Jennifer Rarden for making my manuscript so much better.

A big hug for my biggest cheerleader and believing in me, my husband, Michael. I love you.

My readers, thank you from the bottom of my heart for taking the time to enter my little world of Wings Falls and its characters. Your kind words keep me going.

Most of all a huge thank you to Gemma Halliday for publishing my Samantha Davies series and making my dream come true. I will be forever grateful.

CHAPTER ONE

"How about here?"

"Maybe next to Rudolph." I pointed to the plastic, red-nosed reindeer ornament I had hung on my Christmas tree. "My parents bought him for my first Christmas."

"Your wish is my command." Hank Johnson, my boyfriend, carefully placed a delicate gold-winged angel next to Rudolph then reached over with his strong, calloused fingers and tucked a strand of curly brown hair behind my ear that had fallen over my eyes. Next, he leaned down and kissed me. I grabbed on to his wide shoulders for fear my legs would collapse from the searing heat of his kiss.

I stepped back from his embrace to catch my breath and glanced at my Timex watch. My parents gave it to me years ago as a graduation present. Despite its age, it still kept on ticking. "I guess we should start getting ready to pick up Mom and Dad at the airport. Their plane will arrive in a little over an hour."

"Do you want to clean up these boxes before we go?" Hank pointed to the open ornament boxes scattered on my sofa, chairs, and the floor of my living room. We'd spent the better part of the afternoon decorating my Christmas tree and house.

I loved the Christmas holidays, but not so much all the fuss and muss that went with them. "I guess we should. I don't want Mom to think I'm not taking proper care of the home they gifted me." She'd always kept it neat as a pin. At any unexpected moment, it could have passed the white glove test. Unfortunately, I wasn't as devoted a housekeeper as her. There had been times when my dust bunnies had morphed into dust elephants.

After I divorced my cheating ex, George, my parents signed my childhood home over to me and retired to Florida to enjoy the sunshine and warm weather. Since they'd moved south a little over five years ago, they'd flown home only a few times. We kept in touch with weekly phone calls, but they preferred the Florida winters to the cold and snowy ones of upstate New York. I glanced out my front living room window and noticed a few white flakes floating down from the gray skies.

With my hands on my hips, I gave the tree a critical look. I felt sure my parents would love it. "So, what do you think of our afternoon's work?" I asked Hank. He was busy loading empty ornament boxes into plastic bins.

He stopped his efforts and glanced towards the tree. "I think it's beautiful—just like you."

His compliment caused a rush of heat to flush my cheeks. After a year and half of dating him, I was still getting used to his kind words. Praise had been few and far between in the twenty-five years I had been married to George.

"What do you say about our handiwork, Porkchop?" Hank asked my reddish-brown dachshund, who lay on the floor playing with a wad of tissue paper.

Woof, woof, Porkchop replied.

Hank and I both laughed.

"I'm going to interpret his barks to mean he approves," I said, placing an empty ornament box into a bin on top of the ones Hank had already placed inside.

As I gazed around the room at the decorations on display, fond memories of my childhood growing up in this house flooded me. Tears threatened to escape my eyes. I was overcome with visions of me hanging my stocking on the fireplace mantle and rushing down the hall from my bedroom to see what Santa Claus had left under the tree on Christmas morning.

Hank reached for my hand and led me over to the sofa. He moved the empty ornament boxes to the trunk that served as my coffee table. "Here. Sit. Tell me what you're thinking."

I settled myself onto the chintz-covered sofa, swiped at the tears that threatened to fall with the back of my hand, and then nestled into Hank's arms. The warmth of his body wrapped around me was comforting. Porkchop jumped up on the sofa and settled himself next to me. I gazed into the roaring fire Hank had made in the fireplace when he'd arrived at my house this morning.

"Oh, I was strolling down memory lane, remembering Christmases past." I glanced up at him. "I bet with seven kids in your family, you had some very lively Christmases."

Hank chuckled. "Lively? More like bedlam. How my mom handled all of us, I don't know."

I joined in his laughter. "She must have been a saint rearing all of you on her own." Hank's father was an Albany fireman who died in the line of duty, leaving Hank's mom to raise seven children by herself.

"Yeah, I agree," Hank said with a nod. He pointed to the window I'd glanced out of earlier. "Let me put these bins back in your attic, and then we'd better head out for the airport. The snow isn't much now, but you never know what it will be like by the time your folks' flight lands."

I pushed myself off the sofa. "You're right. I love a white Christmas, but I could do with no snow until after Mom and Dad are safely here. Let me help you, and then I'll see to Porkchop before we go."

Hank kissed the top of my head. "You take care of Porkie, and I'll put the bins away. First, I'd better call Aaron and see how Nina is doing."

Aaron was Hank's younger brother. He'd moved in with Hank about a year ago. His mother had sent him north to live with Hank to get away from a rough crowd in Albany he was hanging around. She'd hoped since Hank was a detective with the Wings Falls Police Department, my hometown, it would be a good influence on him. Thankfully, it was. Nina, Hank's miniature bulldog—well, she was the other love of both Hank's and Porkchop's lives.

"Okay," I said. "Come on, Porkie. Do you want some kibble before Hank and I leave for the airport?" My answer was a bark and his tail wagging as if it were a flag caught in a gale-force wind.

Porkchop trotted next to me into the kitchen. I glanced around the room. It was stuck in the eighties, when my parents last did a remodel. Coppertone was okay with me, as the kitchen held memories of me sitting at the table after school, enjoying a glass of chocolate milk and a plate of chocolate chip cookies. Nope, the people on those TV home remodeling shows can have their "gut" jobs. I'll settle for my memories. I reached up into a maple cabinet over the Formica counter and pulled down Porkchop's bag of kibble. Porkie hopped with joy as he heard his food plink into his bone-shaped bowl. You'd think I hadn't fed him in days the way he gobbled it down.

After he'd devoured his food, I asked, "Okay? Finished, boy? How about a romp around the backyard before Hank and I leave?"

He followed me to the kitchen door. As I opened it, a blast of cold air and snow flurries whooshed into the kitchen. Porkchop stood at the open door, reluctant to waddle down the steps to my fenced-in backyard. "I know, sweetie. Going out to do your business in this weather isn't your favorite thing. But Hank shoveled you a path so your belly won't drag in the snow."

My dog cocked his head as if he understood every word I said. At times, I believed he did.

Reluctantly, Porkchop descended the three cement steps to the ground. His feet had no more touched the snow-covered lawn before he squatted and then was ready to come back inside. Unlike in the summer, when he would linger to sniff out squirrels or chipmunks. He did his thing then raced up the steps and into the kitchen, shaking off the snowflakes melting on his fur.

I locked the kitchen door then walked back into the living room.

Hank stood next to the Christmas tree with my down coat over his arm. "It's a beautiful tree. We did a great job decorating, if I do say so myself."

I reached up and tucked back the lock of curly brown hair that had fallen over his forehead. "It looks beautiful," I whispered against his lips.

His crystal-blue eyes glazed over with desire. "Not half as beautiful as you."

I drew in a ragged breath. "Oh, my. We'd better stop there, or we'll miss my parents' plane."

Hank stepped back and held my coat out for me to slip on. "Yep, you're right. I don't want to make a bad first impression on them."

Although we'd been dating for a while, my parents had yet to meet Hank. When they flew home last year, he was working and didn't have the chance to meet them. Unlike many other professions, police officers often worked holidays so we citizens could enjoy a safe and carefree celebration.

"Okay, let's hit the road before they become too snow-covered," Hank said, opening the front door for me.

A blast of light and the tune "Here Comes Santa Claus" hit me as I descended the front steps of my house. "Oh, my. Mr. Sayers has outdone himself this year. Wait until my dad sees this. Like my memaw Parker would say. 'he'll be madder than a wet hen'."

CHAPTER TWO

———

Hank held my arm as we walked to his Jeep. The snow was deepening. "I don't remember him putting on this much of a production last year."

"No, I heard last year he was suffering from a bout of the flu, so he couldn't decorate his house like he usually does." Neighborhood gossip was a font of information.

Hank opened the passenger door of his Jeep. I climbed inside, settled myself on the seat, and tucked my red Vera Bradley purse next to me. Designer purses were a weakness of mine. He closed the door behind me and walked over to the driver's side. Once inside, he glanced over at my neighbor's house. "It really is quite a display. The whole house is outlined in lights. It looks like every tree in the front yard is wrapped in lights, too. Is he lugging out a life-sized Rudolph?"

I turned in my seat towards my neighbor's yard. "Yep, that would be my favorite reindeer. Before Mr. Sayers is done, Rudolph will be joined by at least thirty other plastic and blowup figures. Frosty the Snowman, the Grinch, gingerbread men and women, towering candy canes, and Santa and his sleigh will be just a few of the characters on his lawn."

"Wow. I'm sure it's something to behold. I'm as big a fan of Christmas music as the next person, but I don't think I'd like it blasted as loud as your neighbor does. Come January, I'd hate to have the guy's electric bill. So, tell me, why would your dad have a fit over his Christmas display? Does he have a bit of the Grinch in him?" Hank gave Rudolph one last glance then put his car into reverse.

I waggled my fingers in front of the car's heater to soak up the warmth blasting from the vents. "No, Dad and Mr. Sayers have been feuding for as long as I can remember. I think it all goes back to when they were in high school together."

Hank's eyebrows rose. "High school? You've got to be kidding me. Isn't that a long time to hold a grudge? What happened to set it off?" He put the car in Drive, and we headed towards the airport.

"Mom" was my one-word answer.

Hank looked at me as we stopped at a red light. "Your mother? What did she do? Dump one guy for the other?"

I nodded. Melting snow dripped off the knit hat I had pulled over my curly brown hair before we left the house. "Yep. Apparently both men pursued my mom their senior year in high school. She dated Mr. Sayers briefly, but then Dad asked her out, and well, that was the end for dear Mr. Sayers. It's not like he and Mom were going steady or anything. From the little Mom's told me about her high school days, she'd only had a couple of dates with him, but I guess he read more into the dates than what was there."

"Poor fella. Unrequited love." The light changed to green, bringing Hank's attention back onto the snow-covered road ahead of him.

I stared out the window at the falling snow. The wipers were having a tough time keeping the windshield clear of the white stuff. "Poor fellow? He even moved north from Hainted Hollar, Tennessee where they all grew up so he could be near Mom. I think he hoped my parents would divorce or, worse yet, something drastic might happen to my dad so he could step in and 'console' Mom."

Hank side-eyed me. "Console your mother? Now I can see why your dad and Mr. Sayers wouldn't be BFF's. I'd be pretty upset if your ex moved next door to be near you."

A smile spread across my face. "Not going to happen. The only dealings I have with him are strictly business." George and I still co-owned a business, the Do Drop Inn Funeral Parlor. Although he may have been the undertaker, I was the one who provided the money when we were first married—from an inheritance—to purchase the business. Now, I wait for my monthly check from the business's proceeds.

"At least the traffic isn't too bad tonight. The weather must be keeping people in. Even though we're driving slower than usual because of the snow, we should be at the airport in plenty of time before your parents' plane lands. Have you gotten any notification on your phone as to whether it's delayed or not?" Hank asked.

I dug into my purse for my phone. I'd finally had to upgrade from my trusty flip phone when I forgot to take it out of the pocket of my jeans before washing them. Soap suds and flip phones don't mix. I tapped the app for the Albany Airport. "The app says all planes are on time. The folks staying home are smart. If it weren't for my parents' coming in tonight, I'd suggest we stay home cuddled up on the sofa, sipping hot chocolate and enjoying a roaring fire."

A smile tugged at Hank's handsome face. "I could go with your plan. Keep it in mind for when your folks fly back to Florida."

"Oh, I will. Look, there's the exit for the airport." I pointed to the green road sign announcing our exit.

Hank clicked on the car's turn signal and followed the signs for the airport. Within minutes, we pulled into the airport's parking garage and entered the airport itself. Although the airport served New York's Capital Region, by big city standards, it was fairly small and easy to get around. One waiting area served all incoming flights. No rushing to find the arrival gate. I glanced at my watch as Hank and I each claimed one of the molded plastic seats. "We've got about ten minutes to wait until their plane arrives. Let's relax and people watch."

"People watch?" Hank asked as he unbuttoned the front of his down coat.

"Yeah, you know, try and guess where the people coming through those doors are going? I used to do it all the time when I came to the airport with Mom and Dad when we picked up Memaw Parker on one of her visits."

Memaw was my mom's mom. Every once in a while, Mom had been able to convince her to fly north for a visit, but those were few and far between. Usually, Mom, Dad, and I would pile into our station wagon for the long trip south to my grandparents' farm for a visit. They'd leave me there to spend the summer running through the fields with my Southern Belle cousin, Candie Parker-Hogan. Memaw and Grandpop had raised her since she was five years old, after her parents were killed in an automobile accident. Both of us being an only child, Candie and I treasured those summer months together. We were closer than most sisters, so I was thrilled when she moved north about fifteen years ago to Wings Falls. A shake of my head returned me to the present. I pointed towards the swinging doors that separated the waiting room from the arriving planes.

Hank chuckled. "Okay, I'm game. How about that person?" He nodded towards a gentleman in a business suit with an overcoat slung across his arm. He carried a reusable shopping bag bursting with wrapped presents.

"Oh, he's easy. He's a dad returning from a business trip with a bag full of presents for his kids." As if to prove me right, a young boy and girl ran towards him yelling, "Daddy! Daddy!" Right behind them walked a tall, slim blonde woman who the gentleman, after hugging his children, embraced then placed a lingering kiss on her lips.

"I bet those two are going to have a great celebration tonight after they tuck the kids in bed."

I poked Hank in the side. "Jealous?"

"You bet I am," he said, rubbing his side. "What do you make of the long-haired fellow with the bored look and a backpack?"

"Easy-peasy. He's a college student, home on winter break, but he'd rather spend it with his buddies drinking beer. Since Mom and Dad are paying his way through college, he doesn't want to upset them and skip Christmas at home."

Hank frowned. "You think so?"

"Sure. Don't you remember when you were in college? Your parents were so uncool. Hanging out with your friends was the place to be," I said, glancing past the college student at the digital display mounted on the wall in front of us that announced all airplane arrivals. "Oh look, my parents' plane has landed."

No sooner had I said those words than the metal doors swung open and what walked through caused me to blink my eyes and my mouth to drop open in disbelief.

CHAPTER THREE

I rose from my seat and started towards the man and woman I called Mom and Dad, barely able to believe my eyes.

"Your parents?" Hank whispered out of the side of his mouth.

"Yeah. Umm, that is, I think so," I replied. "Mom? Dad?" I asked as I approached the couple laden with carry-on bags.

"Sam!" the petite woman screeched as she scurried towards me, plastic bags slapping against her legs.

The gentleman, wearing sunglasses and a backwards ball cap, walked towards Hank with his hand outstretched in greeting. "Your main squeeze, I presume?" he asked, turning towards me while pumping Hank's hand.

What had happened to the parents I had waved goodbye to in this very same airport last Christmas? My staid mother? Well, okay, my dad was always a rogue character—large, brash, and burly—but my mom? I couldn't believe her transformation. Before me stood a woman whose former brown hair streaked with gray was now bleached platinum blonde. She'd replaced the muumuu she wore when she boarded her flight south with skintight leopard print leggings and a silky tunic top. She could barely balance herself on four-inch-high black platform sandals.

"What do you think?" she asked. When she reached me, she placed her bags on the floor and performed a pirouette, patting the new swingy hairdo that skimmed her shoulders.

"I'm speechless." And I truly was. Where was the apron-clad mom who baked chocolate chip cookies and served them to me along with a glass of milk when I came home from school? I pulled this new version of my mom into a hug.

"I needed a change. So, I thought, why not live out my wildest fantasies? We're only on this earth for a short while. Heck, tomorrow could be the big one for us. You never know at your dad's and my age."

My heart skipped a beat as I stepped back from her embrace. I looked into her green eyes, the same color as mine. "Wait a minute. Are you and Dad all right? This new look…" I flicked my hand up and down her body. "It isn't because you're ill, is it?"

Mom laughed. "Heavens no. Your father and I are fit as ever. We felt like a change, so why not now?"

I blew out a sigh of relief. It ruffled the bangs that had escaped my knit hat.

I glanced over at my dad. While Mom's appearance was a drastic change from her norm, he hadn't changed one bit. For his trip north, he wore what would have been more appropriate for sharing cocktails on his lanai with their friends Marge and Herb Feinstein. Just taking in his pink shorts and palm tree–printed, short-sleeve cotton shirt caused my teeth to chatter.

"Come here and give your dad a big hug, my little Muffin," Dad said, spreading his arms wide. His booming voice carried throughout the waiting area, causing heads to turn in our direction.

Hank's dark eyebrows rose. He whispered, "Little Muffin?"

I had the feeling I'd be getting some ribbing from him because of my dad's pet name for me. That was okay. I was a big girl and could take it.

Dad enfolded me in his muscled arms, the warmth of which flooded me with memories of a treasured childhood, knowing he was the man who would brush away my tears and make my boo-boos all right. I laid my head against his chest and breathed in the familiar scent of the bay rum aftershave he had patted on his face.

Dad looked down at me. "How is everything going? Is your fellow treating you right?"

I glanced over at Hank as he took in my exchange with my dad. I stepped out of my dad's arms and reached for Hank's hand. "Fine, Dad. Perfect, in fact."

"You let me know if he doesn't. Even though I've moved to Florida, I still know people who could take care of him." Dad winked at Mom, who stood next to us. "If you know what I mean."

Mom swatted Dad's arm. "Now, Chuck, don't go giving Hank the wrong impression. He's a member of the Wings Falls Police, after all."

"Babs, I don't care if he's the President of the United States. No one messes with my little Muffin, here." Dad flipped his thumb in my direction.

Behind Dad's back, Hank mouthed, *He knows people who could take care of me?*

I sent him a weak smile and shrugged. I'd have to explain to him later that my dad was a lot of bluster, although I'd never say such to Dad. I gulped, remembering how it was all I could do to keep Dad's temper in check when my ex, George, asked me for a divorce after we'd been married for twenty-five years.

"Sir, are you set to get your luggage from baggage claim?" Hank asked my dad.

Hank stumbled forward when Dad slapped him on the back. "Sure, son. Lead the way."

Hank held out his hand for the duffel bag Dad gripped in his hand while I picked two of the three plastic shopping bags off the floor Mom had placed there. I almost collapsed under their weight. "Mom, what do you have in these bags?"

"Only a few presents. I didn't want to forget any of my northern friends," she said, tottering along beside me. I prayed she didn't twist her ankle walking on her platform shoes. I worried about her spending the holiday in the Wings Falls Hospital with a broken ankle or worse.

Within minutes, we arrived at the baggage claim area. Hank turned to me. "Let me have those bags, and I'll go get my Jeep. After you retrieve your parents' luggage from the carousel, meet me out front."

I leaned up and kissed him. "Will do. I know we must be quick. The airport police won't let you idle outside for too long."

Dad overheard our conversation. "Can't you flash your badge at one of your buddies so we can take our time? I saw a pub on the way down the escalator. Maybe we could park our luggage in a locker and stop in for a brewski before we head home?"

My mouth dropped open. Where was the responsible dad who had raised me? What had happened since he'd moved south? Both he and Mom had turned into what my memaw used to call "party animals."

Hank shook his head. "Sorry, Mr. Reynolds, but I won't take advantage of my job."

My heart swelled with pride. Hank was right. What my dad had asked of him was unethical, and my guy was a very moral person.

"Dad, I have Trail's Head chilling in the fridge at home. I'll open one up for you when we get there," I said, mentioning Hank's favorite beer I kept on hand for him.

Mom patted Dad's arm. "Chuck, Sam's right. It's been a long day, and my feet are killing me. I want to get home and put them up."

I only had to look at Mom's shoes and my feet hurt, and they were twenty years younger than hers.

As soon as Hank had left to retrieve his car, Mom leaned over to me and whispered, "He's a keeper and cute, too."

"I hear you, Babs, and I have to agree. Sam's fella is a real gentleman and seems to be an all-right guy."

I smiled, happy to hear my parents giving Hank their stamp of approval. I may be in my midfifties, but them liking my boyfriend meant a lot to me.

*   *   *

"Woo-wee, what a ride home," Dad proclaimed from the back seat of the Jeep as we pulled into my snow-covered driveway.

"You did a great job, getting us home with all that snow coming down, Hank," Mom said, leaning up from the back seat and patting him on the shoulder.

Hank switched off his car and pulled the key out of the ignition. "Johnson's Taxi at your service, guaranteed door-to-door delivery."

We all laughed at Hank's joke.

Dad swung his door open and stretched then shook his fist in the direction of Theo Sayers's front yard. "What's the jerk think he's doing? Those lights are going to keep me up all night. Why, an alien could see them on Mars. I'm going to give him a piece of my mind in the morning. And the music he has blaring from his outdoor speakers would cause a person to go deaf."

CHAPTER FOUR

"Your tree is beautiful, sweetheart," my mom declared as she sipped a glass of chardonnay and admired the tree Hank and I had decorated. The ornaments twinkled against the multicolored lights.

"Damn straight," my dad started to say.

"Chuck, you're not with your pool-playing buddies now. This is your daughter you're talking to," my mom admonished.

"Sorry, Muffin. Darn straight. It's a beauty." He pointed towards the tree with his promised bottle of Trail's Head.

Hank sat on the sofa with Porkchop cuddled up next to him. My pup leaned into the scratchies his bestie was bestowing on him. Hank smiled at me then pushed himself off the sofa. "I'd better head out. There's a break in the storm. I'm sure Nina misses me, and Aaron probably has better things to do than babysit my pooch."

My dad raised his bushy eyebrows. "Who's Nina and Aaron? He looked at me. "This fellow isn't two-timing you, is he?"

I laughed. "No, Dad. Nina is his bulldog, and Aaron is his younger brother who lives with him."

A wine-induced smile spread across Mom's face. Like me, she was a cheap date. Two glasses were her limit, and she was nursing number two and a half. "Chuck, isn't that sweet. His brother is living with him and he's a dog-daddy."

Yep, what with having an exhausting day and wine on top of it, Mom was definitely at her limit.

"I'll see you to the door," I said, pushing my tired self off the wing chair that sat next to the fireplace.

Hank opened the closet next to my front door and reached in for his down coat. After he'd slipped it on and zipped it, I stood on tiptoes and tugged the collar up around his ears. "You did a wonderful job impressing my parents today."

He gathered me into his arms. "Have I done the same for their daughter?" he asked against my lips before planting a warm kiss on them.

I clung to the sleeves of his coat. "Oh, yes, you certainly have."

Hank turned and opened the front door, and a blast of cold air swooshed into the entryway.

"Drive carefully, and don't forget tomorrow night is the party," I called after him. I lingered in the doorway, shivering, and watched his car back out of my driveway. When I could no longer see the glow from his car's lights, I slowly closed the door and rested my forehead against it, already missing him. Finally, I heaved a sigh and walked back into the living room, where my parents sat on the sofa admiring Hank's and my tree decorating.

Mom patted the sofa cushion next to her. "Come sit with your mom and dad before we all head off to bed."

I did as I was asked and settled on the sofa. Porkchop ambled over and jumped up onto my lap. I stroked his soft fur and gazed at the beautiful tree. The balsam scent filling the room was one of my favorites. It conjured up memories of Christmases past.

"You love him, don't you, sweetheart?"

My mom's comment drew me back to the present. "With all my heart, Mom."

She slid an arm over my shoulder and drew me closer to her side. "Your father and I are so happy for you. We could tell from your weekly phone calls you were genuinely happy. I could hear it in the sound of your voice."

I leaned back on the sofa and gently squeezed Mom's hand. "Oh, Mom, Hank is such a good man, and he makes me happy. Even better, he makes me whole. I don't need a man to do that, but when he's not with me, I feel as if a piece of me is missing."

Mom nodded then reached over for Dad's hand. She raised it to her lips and gently placed a kiss on the weathered back of his hand. A hand that had worked hard to feed and clothe his family. A hand that, through years of working at the local landfill, made sure his small family had a roof over its head. "He reminds me a lot of your dad, a good man."

"Ahh, Babs, you're going to make me blush," Dad said, using his shortened version of Mom's name. A term of endearment only he was allowed to use. "But I have to agree with you, our little

Muffin has found a winner in Hank. Someone I would feel proud to have as my son-in-law."

I jerked up in my seat. "Whoa, don't even go there, Dad. Hank and I haven't even mentioned the 'm' word. And I don't see us doing so anytime soon. One marriage was enough for me."

Porkchop stirred on my lap. I ran a shaking hand over his back.

"Sam, your marriage to George may not have worked, but don't shut out a future with Hank," Mom said, placing a hand on my cheek.

"Mom, I thought my marriage to George would last forever, until I found him involved with the secretary of our business." Porkchop growled when I mentioned George's name. He was a lot wiser than I was. He never cottoned up to my ex. He growled whenever George came near me. But he loved Hank. His tail wagged like a metronome gone crazy when Hank was over. I took that to be a big plus for my boyfriend.

"Muffin, I heard you mention a Christmas party to Hank. What's this party about?" Dad asked then took a sip of his beer.

"Oh, yes, I'm going to host this year's Loopy Lady Christmas party. You know, the rug hooking group I belong to. It's tomorrow night." We Loopy Ladies loved to have a good time, and tomorrow night should be no exception.

Mom clapped her hands. "Oh, goodie. I love those ladies. They are such fun. I was hoping you'd have some sort of holiday celebration, so I packed a few outfits for the occasion."

With my mom's new look, I could only imagine what *that* would be.

"This isn't going to be a hen party, is it? I might have to hang out at Maxwell's Pub for the evening if it is." Maxwell's was a favorite local watering hole, especially on Tuesday dart night.

"No, Dad, the ladies are all bringing their spouses or significant others. You'll know most of the men and can hang with them." There were twelve of us Loopy Ladies, and if they all brought their plus ones, my house would be busting at the seams.

Dad frowned. "You didn't invite your crazy neighbor, did you? If so, I'm out of here for the evening."

"I hope you're not talking about Hank's aunt Gladys, but if you mean Mr. Sayers, no I didn't. I know how you two get along like oil and water."

Dad tried to stifle a loud yawn with one of his large hands. "Babs, I don't know about you, but I'm bushed. I'm heading off to bed." He stood then leaned over and kissed the top of my head. "Night, Muffin. I'll see you in the morning. That is, if I can get any sleep with all those blasted lights flashing from next door. He should be reported to the police for disturbing the peace or, at least, disturbing my sleep. I'm going to mention it to Hank when I see him tomorrow."

I groaned silently. I hoped Hank could survive my parents' visit.

"Chuck, everything will be fine. We'll draw the curtains in our bedroom. They should block out most of the light," Mom said, leaning over to kiss my cheek. "See you in the morning. I'm looking forward to the party tomorrow night. I'll help in any way I can."

"That will be great, Mom, but Candie and Mark are coming over early to lend a hand. And Hank will be here, too." Mark was Candie's husband and the mayor of Wings Falls.

Mom frowned. "What are you going to serve? Your culinary skills aren't the best."

I did a mental eyeroll. So what if Porkchop fared better in the kitchen than me? I could bake a mean frozen pizza.

"It's a potluck, so everyone will bring something to share. I'm going to provide the beverages—you know, beer, wine, and an eggnog punch." *That* I could handle. I might even add a little something to the eggnog to liven it up.

"Okay, sweetheart. I'll see you in the morning." Mom yawned and headed down the hall towards the bedrooms.

"I'll be right behind you. I'm going to let Porkchop out to do his business and turn off the Christmas tree lights."

At the mention of his name, Porkchop raised his head. His slim tail thumped against the sofa cushion. He jumped off the sofa and trotted behind me towards the kitchen's back door. "Grandma Got Run Over by a Reindeer" hit my ears when I opened it. I hoped Mr. Sayers would shut off the music blaring from his outdoor speaker soon, or Dad would be in a Grinch of a mood come morning if the holiday tunes kept him up all night.

CHAPTER FIVE

Dad shuffled into the kitchen rubbing his eyes. From the way his gray hair stood on end, he looked like he'd had a restless night. Porkchop looked up from his morning bowl of kibble and wagged his tail in greeting.

"Morning, Dad. Would you like a cup of coffee? I have bagels, or if you'd like, while you and Mom were sleeping, I did a quick run to Doughnut Haven and bought a dozen assorted doughnuts." I lifted the lid of the box containing the doughnuts. "Look. There's Boston Crème, jelly filled, and chocolate glazed. Your favorites." Like me, Dad was a sucker for a fresh doughnut.

His eyes widened in anticipation. "Muffin, you sure know the way to a man's heart." He reached into the box and pulled out a jelly filled. I laughed as the powdered sugar coating the doughnut sprinkled onto his unshaven chin.

"Here," I said, handing him a paper napkin and plate.

He accepted them then pulled out a chair at the kitchen table and sat. I placed a mug of coffee in front of him and joined him at the table with my own cup and a paper plate with a chocolate glazed resting on it.

Dad stirred sugar and cream into his coffee. "So, Muffin, this Hank fellow looks like a good guy. Are you really in love with him?"

The coffee in my mug splashed over the side as I jerked back at my dad's blunt question. Porkchop ambled over to the table and sniffed around for any dropped crumbs he felt he *had* to lick off the floor. He was better than any vacuum. "Umm, well, Dad, you're right, he's a good guy, and yes, I am in love with him." I bit into my doughnut, hoping to forestall any more conversation about my love life.

Dad took a sip of his coffee and reached into the box for another doughnut. "Other than the few things you'd mention in your weekly phone calls, you haven't told your mother and me a whole lot about him. How come?"

I stared into my cup of steaming coffee. It appeared that my munching on a doughnut wasn't going to stop Dad's questions. Why hadn't I told my parents all about Hank? Was I embarrassed that in my middle fifties, I had finally found true love? Was I afraid if our relationship didn't work out after my unsuccessful marriage to George, it would be another big disaster in my life? Was I superstitious that if I told Mom and Dad about how serious my relationship with Hank was, I would jinx it?

I was acting silly. Since Wings Falls was a small town, most of the people who lived here knew Hank and I were a couple. I was sure the gossip hotline was up to speed about a certain Jeep parked in my driveway late into the night. No, I was guessing it had more to do with my stubbornness. Being an only child, my parents had showered me with love but also kept me wrapped in a protective cocoon, shielded from all that could harm me. I knew they'd want to protect me from any heartache if they felt Hank would in any way hurt me as George had.

"There's not much to say. Hank's a detective on the Wings Falls Police force, has a mini bulldog named Nina, who I think Porkchop is in love with, and I happen to love her owner, Hank." I hoped that answered Dad's questions about our relationship.

Dad reached across the table and patted my hand. "Muffin, you've got a good head on your shoulders. Your mom and I know you wouldn't fall for any fool, and if Hank is worthy of your love, then he's okay with us."

I got up from the table and walked over to him. I leaned down and gave my dad a hug then whispered into his ear. "I love you, Dad."

"What's going on here? Do I smell fresh coffee? Oh, oh, are those doughnuts I see on the counter?" Mom stood in the doorway of the kitchen.

I hurried over to the counter and lifted out a chocolate glazed from the box. I joined her and handed her a paper plate and napkin. "Mom, have a seat and I'll pour you a mug of coffee."

"Okay. We've a lot to do today to get ready for your party tonight." Mom tugged the sash on her leopard-print satin robe then patted her bleached-blonde hair she'd rolled up in pink foam curlers. I still wasn't used to this new version of my mom. She leaned over and planted a kiss on Dad's cheek before taking a seat. "Did you ever get any sleep, Chuck? Thank you, dear," she said as I placed the coffee in front of her. "Your poor dad tossed and turned half the night, what with Theo's music blasting and his lights flashing in our window."

"*Humpf.* Not much. The man should be arrested for disturbing the peace. Haven't your neighbors complained? What about Gladys? I doubt she's too happy with all this nonsense." Dad nodded in the direction of her house.

Gladys, my other next-door neighbor and fellow Loopy Lady, was Hank's octogenarian aunt. "No, Dad, she hasn't complained. Probably because she usually has her police scanner blaring most of the night, too."

"Bunch of crazies. I swear you live next to a bunch of crazies," Dad repeated, shaking his head.

My brick, ranch-style house sat near the end of a tree-lined street. Like mine, most of the houses were built in the fifties. It was a neighborhood where folks raised their families, visited for coffee, and watched out for each other. Most everyone got along except for the occasional odd duck like Theo Sayers. Mr. Sayers was a semi-retired reporter for the *Tribune*, our local newspaper. He and my dad rubbed each other the wrong way, and I had the feeling it went deeper than an unrequited love. Mr. Sayers was married, but over the years I'd gotten the impression it wasn't a happy marriage. Maybe, his wife, Rosa, had resented living next to his true love, my mom. All I knew was they were never invited over to our house for the yearly barbeque my folks hosted for the neighbors while I was growing up.

I took a last sip of my coffee then rose from my chair and put the dirty mug in the dishwasher. I picked up the coffeepot and pointed it towards my parents. "There's a little left. Anyone want to finish it off?"

Both Mom and Dad shook their heads.

"I'll pass," Dad said, swiping a napkin over his lips.

"Me, too," Mom said, getting up from her seat. "I'm going to check and see what I brought with me that I can wear to the party tonight. I packed at least three outfits to pick from."

"Three?" I asked, raising my eyebrows. I did a mental inventory of my closet and thought of my choices. I had planned on a red and green striped sweater, pairing it with a pair of green skinny pants. Maybe I should rethink my plan. I didn't want to look like one of Santa's elves.

* * *

A knock sounded on my front door. The guests had started to arrive.

"I'll get it. You finish what you're doing."

I glanced up from the tub of ice sitting on the end of the buffet in my dining room. I was arranging bottles of beer next to the wine I had cooling in it. "Thank you," I said to Hank as he walked towards the door. Nina and Porkchop trotted behind him. Porkchop sported a red bowtie, while Nina was styling with a ruffed, sparkly green skirt around her middle that I had bought for her. I smiled. Hank and I spoiled our fur babies something fierce.

I caught my reflection in the mirror hanging over the buffet. I'd cleaned up pretty good if I said so myself, and from the look in Hank's eyes when I'd opened the front door to him this evening, I felt he agreed with my assessment. I'd changed my wardrobe choice from the Santa's elf lookalike to a silky red blouse and a pair of black velvet slacks that clung in all the right places. My curly brown hair hung in soft waves over my shoulder, thanks to my trusty blow dryer and paddle brush.

"Hi, sugar. Where do you want me to put this tray of cheese and crackers? Oh, don't Porkchop and Nina look adorable? My Annie and Dixie were snoozing on their beds by the fireplace when Mark and I left home." My Southern Belle cousin, Candie, and her husband, Mark, were the first to arrive. Like me, and much to our Memaw Parker's chagrin, Candie's culinary talents were as limited as mine. The cheese and crackers were her top speed.

I gave my cousin a hug then pointed towards the dining room. "Put them on the table."

After she'd deposited her goodies, Mark helped her out of her lavender wool coat. Any shade of purple was her favorite.

Hank strode into the room. Tonight, if I was busy, his job was door greeter. Since moving to Wings Falls, he and Mark had become good friends. It also helped that since Hank was the lead detective on the town's police force and Mark was the town's mayor, they often worked together. Hank kept Mark informed whenever a major crime happened. Thankfully, the holiday season has been quiet in my hometown so far.

CHAPTER SIX

———

"Here, let me take those," Hank said, holding his hand out for their coats. "Where should I put these, Sam?"

"We'll lay everyone's coats on my bed for the evening." I turned to Mark and Candie. "Would you care for a glass of wine or a beer?"

"A wine for me. Mark, sweetie, what would you like?" Candie slipped her arm through Mark's and led him over to the buffet.

"Beer would be great," he said, gazing into her violet eyes. They had been married for over a year but still acted as if they were in the honeymoon phase of their marriage. But knowing them, I didn't think there would ever be an end to that phase. Candie was engaged eleven times before Mark won her heart. He was a lucky man to claim her as his wife.

Hank walked back into the dining room after depositing Candie's and Mark's coats on my bed.

I nodded towards the living room. "How about we settle in the living room and enjoy the fire before the rest of the Loopy Ladies and their significant others arrive."

Hank had laid a fire in the fireplace earlier in the afternoon. The roaring fire lent a cozy and festive atmosphere to the room.

Candie sat next to Mark on the sofa. She spread her gauzy red skirt out around her. A green sweater studded with red rhinestones completed her outfit. I smiled. There wasn't a rhinestone my cousin didn't like. Bling was her middle name. A sweater with Santa's face topped Mark's green corduroy slacks. They looked like they could be Santa's helpers. My red silk blouse and black slacks looked drab next to their outfits.

"Your home looks so festive. The tree is a beauty. I love the twinkling lights on the mantel," Candie said, glancing about the room.

Hank and I sat in the wing chairs flanking the fireplace. "Yes, I'm lucky Mom and Dad left their Christmas decorations when they moved to Florida. They conjure up fond memories from my childhood every year when I bring them out of the attic and decorate the house."

"Where are Uncle Chuck and Aunt Barbara? You said they were spending the holidays with you. Their flight wasn't canceled, was it?" Candie asked, swirling the wine around her glass.

"No, Dad said they had to make a run to the Shop and Save. He mentioned that something was missing from my Christmas decorations. He said they wouldn't be long." I took a sip of the wine I had poured myself.

As if on cue, Porkchop jumped off his bed next to the fireplace and started to bark. He was better than any alarm system I could have installed. Nina ignored him and continued to sleep on her bed, soaking up the warmth from the fireplace. Moments later, the front door opened and framed Mom with Dad standing behind her.

Candie rose from the sofa and hurried over to them. She pulled both into a hug. "Aunt Barbara, Uncle Chuck, it's been such a long time. How are you? I'm so glad to see you." She stepped back and looked at my dad. "Uncle Chuck, how is your hip?" He'd missed Candie and Mark's wedding because he'd undergone a hip replacement.

Dad stepped farther into the living room. "Fine, my little Southern charmer." He leaned over and planted a kiss on Candle's smooth porcelain check. "Wait until later, and I'll show your new hubby a trick or two on the dance floor when we roll up the rugs and break out the music."

We all laughed. My dad loved to dance and didn't need any coaxing to take a spin around the room to the sounds of a good song.

Mom held up a small paper bag. "Your dad felt there was something missing in your Christmas décor."

I frowned. I couldn't imagine what. "All the ornament bins are empty." My hand swept the room. Every table held a Christmas decoration. "What did I forget?"

Dad took the paper bag from Mom and reached in and pulled out a sprig of mistletoe. We all laughed. "The holidays aren't complete until you kiss your sweetie under the mistletoe," Dad said, pulling Mom into his arms. He raised the mistletoe over her head, leaned down, and kissed her.

Mom's face was as red as my blouse when she came up for air. She waved a hand in front of her face. "The fireplace has sure warmed up the room."

I chuckled and mumbled, "I don't think the fireplace has anything to do with the rise in the room's temperature."

"Where's some tape so I can hang this?" Dad asked, holding the mistletoe towards me.

"I'll be right back," I said, retreating into the kitchen. I pulled open my junk drawer, where I shoved everything without a specific home of its own. Scotch tape was one of them.

I returned to the living room and handed the tape to my dad.

"How about here?" he asked, holding it up to the archway leading into the dining room.

Mom clapped her hands. "Perfect, Chuck."

"Anything you say, Babs." With Mom's approval, he secured the mistletoe in place. "Anyone else want to give it a spin?" he asked, pointing to the mistletoe.

Candie grabbed Mark's hand and pulled him off the sofa. "Come on, sugar. The mistletoe is waiting for us." She led him under the mistletoe and planted a sizzling kiss on his lips.

When she released him, Mark uttered only one word, "Whoa."

Hank held his hand out to me. His mouth curved into a sexy grin. "Care to give it a go?"

My heartrate . I'd seen that grin before and knew he had more than a kiss in mind. "*Ummm*, sure." I stood and let him guide me over to the mistletoe. When we were under it, I stood on tiptoes and leaned into his lips. A tingle ran through my body as he pressed his lips against mine. Everyone else in the room faded away as I absorbed the heat from his kiss.

"Woo-wee, now that is a kiss."

My eyes snapped open at my cousin's comment as heat flushed my face, but not from Hank's kiss. Now it was from embarrassment. I wasn't one for such a public passionate display of emotion, especially in front of my parents. Although, with my mom's new look and the way I caught my dad gazing at her, I wondered if they weren't on their second honeymoon.

"Come on, Chuck. We'd better change for the party. More guests will be arriving soon," Mom said, tugging at Dad's arm.

As if on cue, there was a knock at the front door. Porkchop barked and followed me to the door. I opened it to find my neighbor, Gladys, and her boyfriend, Frank Gilbert, standing on my porch.

I choked back a laugh as I took in her hair color. Tonight, she had dyed her gray curls red and green. Half of her head was green and the other half red. Although, this shouldn't have surprised me. She usually changed her hair color to coordinate with the season or a particular holiday—red for Valentine's Day, orange for Halloween. Whatever struck her fancy. A headband of twinkling red and green lights was nestled in her curls.

"Hi, Gladys, Frank. Come on in." I reached out for the covered dish she carried in her hands.

"My Pookie Bear loves my stuffed shells, so I whipped up a batch," she said, calling Frank by her pet name for him. Gladys had been married to an Irish seaman years before Frank became her Pookie Bear. In fact, her late husband's ashes were encased in an urn sitting at the helm of his old fishing boat rotting away in her backyard, but she was Italian through and through.

"Hank will take your coats, and I'll set your dish on the dining room table. Help yourselves to a drink. They're on the buffet." I flicked my hand towards the tub holding the drinks.

Gladys and Frank handed their coats over to Hank then made their way into the dining room. Soon other guests started to arrive. Marybeth Higgins came with a tray full of barbeque sliders from her brother Clint's restaurant, the Smiling Pig. Franny Goodway, the owner of Sweetie Pie's Café, although not a Loopy Lady, was ladened with three banana cream pies, to die for. I practically drooled as I helped her place them on the dining room table.

Susan Mayfield and her husband, Brian, the owners of Momma Mia's Italian restaurant, treated the group to a large pan of lasagna. Susan set the lasagna next to pasta dishes, bean salads, and much more. Anira Plum and her husband, Tony, brought a basket of fresh rolls to go with the main dishes.

Hank stood next to me, scanning the array of dishes on the table. "Are we expecting an army to invade your home tonight?"

I laughed. "With all of this food, you'd think so, wouldn't you? But no, we hookers know how to throw a party, and there's always plenty of food. I wonder what's keeping Mom and Dad?"

As if on cue, they entered the living room. At the sight of them, I swallowed back laughter that wanted to escape. Dad wore bright red and green checked slacks, a sweater with a reindeer's face, and a red bow tie dotted with miniature flashing lights.

Mom's outfit rivaled Dad's for being festive. Her legs were encased in green tights decorated with candy canes. For her top, she wore an oversized sweater with a sequin penguin sporting a Santa hat. A green elf's hat was perched atop her blonde hair.

"Hi, everyone. Greetings from sunny Florida," Dad shouted to the gathered crowd.

"Hello, Barbara and Chuck" came right back at them.

The front door opened, and in stepped Herb and Marge Feinstein. "I heard there's a party going on here. Is there room for two more?"

Herb and Marge were my parents' best friends from Florida. In fact, Dad had worked with Herb for over twenty-five years at the local landfill. Both retired at the same time and moved south to enjoy cocktails together on their lanais.

Mom was the first to come out of a stunned state and moved towards the front door to welcome her friends with a hug for each. "When did you two get into town? I didn't know you were coming north. How did you find out about the party?"

Marge smiled. Her silver-gray bob swung about her shoulders. "We stopped at Sweetie Pie's this afternoon, and Franny mentioned it. Our granddaughter, Gabbie, texted us she was going to be home for Christmas, so Herb and I decided to catch a redeye and bunk in with our daughter and make it a real family Christmas."

Dad walked up to Herb and gave him a hearty slap on the back. "Good to see you, buddy. Come on in and pop open a beer."

Herb and Marge followed my parents into the dining room, where they handed their friends a drink.

The door opened one more time, and Santa stepped in.

"Ho, ho, ho," the skinny Santa in a stained red suit and scuffed black boots greeted us.

I gripped Hank's hand. "Oh, no."

CHAPTER SEVEN

———

Hank frowned. "What's the matter? It's Santa. Aren't you happy to see him?" One of his well-shaped eyebrows rose on his forehead. "Have you been a bad girl and you're afraid he's going to tell your parents?"

I shook my head, causing the silk poinsettia I'd tucked over my ear to dislodge and fall to the floor. "I only wish it was that simple." I pointed to the Santa, who strolled about my living room passing out candy canes to my guests. "Santa is my next-door neighbor, Theo Sayers."

Recognition dawned on Hank's face. "Ohhh, he's the infamous neighbor. Do you want me to ask him to leave?"

I bent and picked up my Christmas flower and tucked it back into my hair. "No. Hopefully, he'll behave. I've never had any issues with him. The problem is between him and my parents."

I walked over to Santa to greet him. "Hello, Mr. Sayers. Glad to see you tonight. How is Mrs. Sayers?" I sucked in my breath as alcohol fumes surrounded me when I reached him. Santa must have already been celebrating before he came to my house.

Santa, aka Theo Sayers, paused in making his rounds of my living room, one hand filled with candy canes. He stroked his beard and looked me up and down. I shivered at his lecherous leer. He definitely was not the jolly bearded fellow I visited in the shopping malls of my youth. "Rosa is laid up at home with a headache. I saw you had a holiday gathering and thought I'd spread some cheer. It's that time of year, and I am a professional Santa, you know? I'm the mall's Santa." He placed his hands on his hips and struck a pose in his red suit, hat, and black boots.

My eyes widened at this information, and I wondered if I had a child, if I'd want him or her whispering into this Santa's ear, but that was unfair of me. In all the years I'd lived next to him and his wife, I'd never had any issues with them.

"What are you doing here, Theo? Why don't you slither on back to the spectacle you call your home?"

I turned to see my dad with Mr. Feinstein standing next to him. "Dad, it's okay. Mr. Sayers wants to spread some Christmas cheer. I'm sure as soon as he hands out his candy canes, he'll be on his way. Right, Mr. Sayers?"

I glanced around my living room. Thankfully, most of the Loopy Ladies were busy enjoying the food spread out on my dining room table and not paying attention to us. Their chatter drowned out our discussion. When my eyes came to rest on Candie, though, she raised a questioning eyebrow at me. I shrugged in answer, not sure what was going to happen between the three gentlemen.

"Ho, ho, ho." Unlike my idea of Santa, this Santa had no belly to jiggle when he laughed. "I have a present to deliver to these two gentlemen before I leave." He turned to my dad and Mr. Feinstein. "Your dirty deeds at the landfill are going to make headline news very soon. I have a real scoop you might want to hear before it becomes public."

Dad turned to Mr. Feinstein and frowned. "Do you know what he's jabbering on about, Herb?"

Mr. Feinstein shook his head. "Not a clue, Chuck. Maybe we should go into your den and listen to what he has to say?"

"Okay." He turned to Mr. Sayers. "This had better be good."

"Oh, it is," Mr. Sayers sneered.

As they headed in the direction of my den, Hank, Candie, and Mark walked up to me.

"What was that all about?" Candie asked. "Your dad and Mr. Feinstein didn't look too happy with Santa." Her eyes followed the men as they walked towards my den.

Hank slid an arm over my shoulder and drew me close to him. "I didn't want to butt in, but I have to agree with Candie. From the expression on the guys' faces, it didn't look like anyone was filled with Christmas joy."

I reveled in the feel of his body next to mine. "I'm not sure. Mr. Sayers mentioned something about an article going into the newspaper. He intimated it had to do with Dad and Mr. Feinstein?"

"How would Mr. Sayers know what is being printed in the paper? Is it the *Tribune* we're talking about?" Hank asked, referring to the area's newspaper.

I nodded. "Yes. Mr. Sayers has worked for them forever."

Candie tapped one of her bejeweled fingers to the side of her head then turned towards Mark. "Didn't he write a glowing article about your opponent when you were running for reelection last year? But more information came out about the fellow's shady background, and he was arrested for writing bad checks and using stolen credit cards."

Mark rolled his beer bottle between his hands. "Yes, he's the one. Can't say I'm a fan of his. Mr. Sayers and I have different opinions. I believe that a financial fraudster shouldn't hold the most powerful office in Wings Falls. Mr. Sayers thinks differently. His article almost got a criminal elected as Wings Falls' mayor. Thankfully, the truth came out in the end."

Hank ran his hand up and down my arm as we talked, sending a comforting warmth through me. "Mr. Sayers has to be your parents' age if he went to school with them."

"Yes, they're in their mid-seventies. He's good friends with the newspaper's owner so they throw him an article or two to keep him busy. I guess he wrote one he thinks would be of interest to my dad and Mr. Feinstein." I smiled and said hello to Helen Garber and her husband, Orville, as they walked past me with plates loaded with a sampling of every dish on the table. As usual, Helen's outfit for tonight was as colorful as my Christmas tree. Subtle was not a familiar word to Helen. Her green sweater, adorned with dancing elves, and matching green slacks were bright enough to give Mr. Sayers's front yard decorations a run for their money.

I glanced over to the sofa, where Mom and Mrs. Feinstein sat huddled together talking. They both wore serious looks on their faces and repeatedly glanced towards the den, where their husbands were talking with Mr. Sayers.

"You fool. I'll sue you for slander. We were not involved in that, and if the rag you call a newspaper prints it, we'll see you in court. Right, Herb?"

"You can count me in, Chuck. We had nothing to do with it."

My head, plus all the heads in the room, snapped towards the raised voices coming out of my den.

"Get out of here. Go home, and don't ever step foot in my house again." Dad's raised voice rang through the closed den doors.

A cackle followed Dad's statement. "From what I gather, it ain't your house anymore, Chuckie-Boy. It belongs to your beautiful daughter. She sure does take after her mom. I wonder if she'd fancy an older gentleman like me?"

Hank's body stiffened as he heard Mr. Sayers's crude comment. He took a step towards the den. I tugged on his arm to hold him back. "Ignore him. He's half drunk."

A dark look crossed his handsome face as I felt his arm muscles stiffen under my hands. "No one talks about you that way. No one."

"Hank, leave it to Dad and Mr. Feinstein to handle Mr. Sayers. Their feud has been going on for as long as I can remember. Okay?"

Those words had no more left my mouth than the den doors flew open. Dad and Mr. Feinstein held Mr. Sayers by his arms and marched him towards the front door. Mr. Sayers's feet dangled off the ground.

Gladys jumped up from the wing chair by the fireplace where she'd been enjoying a glass of Chablis and scurried toward the front door. She swung it open for Dad. "I see you have some trash to toss out, Chuck. Let me be of help." The people in the room clapped as she slammed the door shut after them.

A sob drew me towards the dining room. My mother stood by the table. Tears mixed with her mascara ran down her cheeks. Her carefully coiffed hair looked deflated as it hung about her pale face. I hurried over to her and drew her into my arms. "This is all my fault," she sobbed against my shoulder.

"Mom, you're talking nonsense," I said, rubbing my hand in circles against her back. Our roles had reversed now. I remembered how my mother used to rub my back when I was upset about something. Now *I* was trying to calm *her*. "You have done nothing wrong. Mr. Sayers is a bitter old man."

Mom pulled out of my arms and looked up at me. I may not be tall at only five-foot-three, but my mom barely reached five feet. "You don't understand. He's never forgiven me for spurning his advances all those years ago in high school."

Exasperated, I blew out a deep breath and shook my head. "Mom, for him to carry a torch for you all these years, I think, borders on an obsession—and not a very healthy one, either."

"Aunt Barbara, honey, Sam is right. You've never done anything to encourage him. He's just a sicko."

I turned to see Candie standing behind us. Having been engaged eleven times, Candie would know about men and their quirks. The look on her face was one of sympathy and concern. She brushed back a strand of auburn hair that had escaped the loose bun resting on the nape of her neck. She was a true Southern Belle, and not just because of her thick Tennessee accent. Her compassion and sense of concern for other people were instilled in her by our memaw Parker.

The lights in the house suddenly flashed off but blinked back on in seconds.

"*Humph*. I bet that old fool Theo's monstrous light display has caused a power surge in the neighborhood," Gladys said from the living room, where she'd returned to the wing chair by the fireplace and still held court.

The front door burst open. Dad and Mr. Feinstein strode into the living room. Snowflakes swirled in with them.

"Phew. It's snowing pretty hard out there," Dad said, brushing flakes off his shoulders.

"Did you see Mr. Sayers home safely?" I asked. While I didn't want him in my house, I didn't want any harm to come to him, and in his drunken condition, he could stumble and hurt himself.

"We left him in his driveway. It was up to him to navigate the rest of the way to his house," Mr. Feinstein said as he walked into the living room.

"Oh, Herb, that wasn't very nice. I mean, it is the holiday season, after all." Mrs. Feinstein looked up at her husband from the sofa, where she sat shredding a tissue into tiny pieces.

"The heck with all that goodwill stuff, Marge. He certainly wasn't showing any to Chuck and me with his threats."

I frowned. What could Mr. Sayers know that would harm my dad and Mr. Feinstein? "What threats?" I asked.

"Oh, it's nothing. I'm starved, Babs. I need to load up a plate with some of the great food sitting on the dining room table and chow down." Dad waved a hand towards the table.

The evening progressed without any further incidents. It was filled with laughter and good food. Mr. Sayers's visit was all but forgotten until an ear-piercing scream from outside stopped all conversation.

CHAPTER EIGHT

Hank ran out my front door before I could register what was happening. Candie, Mark, and I followed close behind him. A sobbing Rosa Sayers stood in the middle of her front lawn dressed in baggy sweatpants. An oversized sweater hung from her thin shoulders. Snow swirled about her as she pointed a shaking finger towards the middle of her lawn.

"Stand back," Hank shouted as we approached him.

"Hank, what is it?" I asked, wrapping my arms around myself. My silk blouse, which I thought was so sexy earlier, did nothing to ward off the cold seeping through my body. Right now, I'd give anything for my fleece-lined boots and the ratty sweatpants and paint-stained sweatshirt hanging in my bedroom closet.

"Sam, do you have your phone on you? I left mine in my coat pocket," Hank called over to me as I saw him kneel down on the lawn.

"No," I said through chattering teeth.

"Here, you can use mine," Candie said, pulling her bejeweled phone out of her skirt pocket.

I smiled. Everything about my cousin sparkled—even her phone.

Hank stood and walked over to her to retrieve the phone. He punched in a series of numbers. "I have an unresponsive male at…"

"Unresponsive male?" I tried to look past Hank to see what was happening. Did he mean *unresponsive* as in *dead*? I shivered again.

Hank gave the dispatcher the address of where we were. "And notify Doc Cordone." He tapped the phone off and handed it back to Candie before walking back to where he'd been.

I turned to Candie and Mark. "Doc Cordone?"

"Doc is only called out when there's a suspicious death," Candie said, shivering as she clung to Mark's arm.

Mark nodded in agreement. "Hank, what do you have there?" As the mayor of Wings Falls, he'd have to be informed of any death that appeared to be unnatural.

"I think you might want to check this out," Hank said.

On instinct, Candie and I followed Hank and Mark. The front lawn was covered in a liberal dusting of snow. Mrs. Sayers stood in the middle of the lawn where Rudolph had been positioned earlier in the day, though he was now topped over on top of what I assumed was the body in question.

Mark joined Hank at the prone body. Candie and I inched closer to them.

I heard my party guests buzzing behind me on my front porch. I turned, and sure enough, they were huddled together trying to get a glimpse of what had happened on my neighbor's front lawn. I spotted Gladys front and center. The twinkling red and green lights on her headband glowed about her head.

Mr. Sayers's Christmas lights were darkened. I wondered if the power surge we experienced moments ago had blown them out.

"Candie, shine your phone's flashlight in Hank's direction," I directed.

When Candie did as I said, I gasped again at what the phone illuminated. The man on the ground was wearing a Santa suit, and as the light shone across his face, I could clearly see it was Mr. Sayers. Rudolph sat on top of him, and his Santa boots poked out from beneath the reindeer's belly. A string of Christmas lights was wrapped around his neck, and candy canes were shoved into his mouth.

I grabbed Candie's arm. "Candie, that's Mr. Sayers under Rudolph."

Candie nodded. "You're right, sugar. It doesn't look like Santa will be visiting your house again this year."

Sirens screamed down my street, replacing the holiday songs that had earlier blasted from Mr. Sayers's outdoor speakers. Two black and whites screeched to a halt in front of the Sayers's house, followed by an ambulance. Out of the first squad car climbed two officers I'd gotten to know over the last year from being involved in less-than-happy occasions—murders. Officers Reed and March were fairly new to the force but fast becoming an integral part. Officer Reed nodded to Candie and me as he walked up the driveway. The falling snow was a sharp contrast to his dark skin as he approached the body.

The doors of the second car swung open. I frowned when the passenger stepped out—Sargeant Joe Peters. Joe and I tolerated each other. Unfortunately, we had a history going all the way back to kindergarten, and not a good one. It wasn't my fault I reported him to the teacher for peeing in the sand box. I mean, who wanted to play in the sand after he'd christened it? Kids, though, have a long memory and called him "Sandy" all through school. And yes, sometimes I slipped and called him by his dreaded nickname when I was irked with him, especially when he was trying to accuse me of murder, which he had done on more than one occasion.

He flipped on a high-powered flashlight to light his way up the Sayers's driveway. In the glow of the flashlight, I noticed that his face twisted in pain as he limped up the driveway. He appeared to have injured his leg.

From the driver's side of the car emerged a female police officer. She flipped back her blonde ponytail and adjusted her hat then pulled the hem of her jacket around a trim waist.

Candie leaned towards me. "Who's the new officer? She's a real stunner." Because of her job in the mayor's office, she knew most of the Wings Falls police officers, so I was surprised when she didn't recognize the woman climbing out of the squad car. Like Joe and the other officers, Mimi also carried a flashlight that illuminated the area where Mr. Sayers lay. But I was too far away to make out any further details of his death than what the glow of flashlights had shown us, although I didn't know if I really wanted to see any more than I already had.

I shrugged. I was rapidly turning into an ice cube. Again, I wished I'd thought of grabbing my coat as I rushed out the door. "That's Mimi Greensleeves, newly transferred in from Albany."

Officer Greensleeves joined Hank and the other officers. From the bits of conversation I overheard, they were busy discussing what might have happened to Mr. Sayers.

"Like Hank, huh?" Candie asked. Hearing her chattering teeth, I figured she too regretted not nabbing her coat as we rushed out of my house.

"Not quite. Wings Falls Police was in need of a lead detective and recruited Hank from Albany. He was more than ready to leave Albany's busy department for a quieter one."

Candie let out a forced laugh. "Yeah, like he's found it here. Our little town has had a number of murders in the short time he's been here."

I nodded. "Unfortunately, it's true. But Hank mentioned Wings Falls Fire Department was recruiting, and Officer Greensleeves' husband, who worked as a fireman in Albany, applied for the position and was hired."

"Ahhh," Candie laughed. "Once again, Wings Falls scores one on Albany."

I was startled by a voice behind me. "Here, Muffin. No sense freezing your buns off."

"Dad, thanks a bunch," I said, slipping my arms into the sleeves of the coat he held out to me.

"I didn't forget you, Candie." Dad handed my cousin her coat, which she quickly donned.

She leaned up and planted a kiss on Dad's whiskered cheek. "Thanks so much, Uncle Chuck."

Dad wrapped an arm around my shoulder.

"What do you think happened to Mr. Sayers, Dad? Maybe he was checking his Christmas display and got tangled up in a string of lights."

I could feel him shrug. "*Humph*. Who knows, but it couldn't happen to a more deserving guy."

I pulled away from him in shock. I'd never heard my dad say a mean thing about anyone my whole life. Well, maybe he grumbled a little about Mr. Sayers over the years. But nothing anyone would take seriously.

"Dad, what do you mean? What did he do to you that you'd wish him dead?"

My father shook his head. It had started to snow again, and snowflakes fell from his hair. "Nothing, Muffin. Forget what I said. I'm going back into the house and see to your mom. This has gotten her pretty upset."

"Okay, Dad. Thanks for the coats." I hugged him.

"Don't stay out here too long. The two of you could catch a cold. You don't want to ruin your Christmas with the sniffles." Dad gave both Candie and me a kiss on the cheek then turned and walked back up my drive to the house.

"Thank you, Uncle Chuck," Candie called to my dad.

He waved over his shoulder to us as he walked away, but instead of going inside, he stood on the porch with Mr. Feinstein and watched what was happening next door.

I snuggled into my down coat, but a chill still snaked its way up my spine. "What do you think my dad meant when he said, 'it couldn't happen to a more deserving guy'?"

Candie frowned. "I don't know, but if Mr. Sayers's death is suspicious, Uncle Chuck and Mr. Feinstein may become prime suspects."

CHAPTER NINE

I gazed at my cousin with an open mouth. "Candie! How can you say such a thing? You've known my dad all your life. He wouldn't hurt a flea, and neither would Mr. Feinstein. They're best buds."

Candie grasped my ice-cold hand in hers. "Sugar, I know, but there's a house full of people who overheard them arguing tonight, and the next thing we know, Mr. Sayers is lying in the snow run over by a reindeer."

I couldn't help the smile that turned up the corners of my lips. "Yeah, I guess this time *Grandma* got lucky and it wasn't her. But I know neither my dad nor Mr. Feinstein had anything to do with Mr. Sayers's death."

"Sam, you and Candie should go back into the house. I'm afraid I'm going to be tied up here for quite a while."

My head jerked around at the sound of Hank's voice. "How come? He got caught up in a tangle of lights, right? For heaven's sake, they're strewn all over his front lawn." I flicked my hand towards the maze of light strings. "Maybe he wasn't looking where he was walking." My voice sounded desperate, even to me.

Hank pulled me to him. I nestled against him, loving the feel of his arms around me. "Not sure yet. We're checking it out, but there's no reason for you to stand around in the snow, freezing. Go inside and check on your guests. It looks like most of them have retreated back into your house." He nodded to the porch.

The only ones still standing on the porch in the freezing cold were my dad, Mr. Feinstein and, of course, the ever-vigilant Gladys O'Malley. Even her boyfriend, Frank, aka Pookie Bear, had sought the warmth of the indoors.

"Come inside and thaw out," I said to them as I climbed the steps of my front porch.

Gladys pulled the red and white afghan Memaw Parker had crocheted for me around her shoulders. She must have retrieved it from the back of my sofa. "But I don't want to miss what's going on over there." Her red and green curls bobbled as she nodded towards my neighbor's house.

I smiled. Not much escaped her attention. "Gladys, I'm sure you'll catch up on what's going on later when you turn on your police scanner." She listened to it day and night, and being slightly hard of hearing, which she'd deny, the volume was turned up so high most of the neighborhood heard it, too.

I held my front door open for her to enter and then turned to my dad and Mr. Feinstein. "No use you two standing out here getting a cold or worse. Come inside and warm up."

"Okay, Muffin," Dad said as the two of them followed me into the house.

A blast of heat from the fireplace hit me as I stepped inside. The living room, den, and dining room overflowed with my guests munching on the goodies that they brought tonight. I walked over to the roaring fire and held out my hands to thaw them. My fingers tingled as heat seeped into my digits. I was so engrossed with what was happening next door, I hadn't realized how really cold I had become.

"Here, dear, take a sip of this."

I turned to see my mom holding a steaming mug of hot chocolate out to me. "Thanks, Mom," I said, wrapping my fingers around the warm mug. I took a sip and sighed. It hit the spot. I watched as she walked across the room and sat with her friend Marge Feinstein on the sofa. From the frown on their faces, it looked like they were engaged in a serious conversation. Were they discussing Mr. Sayers's demise?

Candie joined me by the fireplace with a mug of her own. "So, what do you think happened?" she asked. The hot chocolate foam left a mustache on her upper lip.

I shrugged. "If I had to guess, I'd say Mr. Sayers tripped in the deepening snow and got tangled up in the maze of electric cords strewn all over his front lawn. He fell and pulled Rudolph down on top of him."

Candie shook her head. Blinking Christmas light bulb earrings slapped against her neck. "Maybe, but how did the wires become wrapped around his neck, and how do you account for the candy canes in his mouth?"

I gulped a mouthful of hot chocolate. It burned my throat as it slid down. "Ouch," I gasped and waved my fingers in front my mouth, trying to cool off my tongue. "I don't know. Maybe he was sucking on them when he fell."

Candie placed a slender hand on my arm. "Are you okay?"

"Yes. Yes. Your questions took me by surprise. I'd assumed it was an accident, but by all the police activity outside, it doesn't appear to have been. Who would have done this to him? I've known the man all my life. Is he a pain? Yes. But one my family has always ignored."

"Until tonight," Candie said, gazing into her mug of hot chocolate, not able to look me in the eye.

My eyes widened. "Meaning?"

Candie looked around my living room. "All of your guests heard and saw your dad and his friend having a heated argument with Mr. Sayers."

A chill ran down my spine, and it wasn't from the cold I'd experienced outside. This was the second time tonight my cousin had made such a comment. "You know Dad and Mr. Feinstein wouldn't harm anyone, let alone kill a person, even someone as disagreeable as Mr. Sayers."

"I know Uncle Chuck wouldn't, but do you know his friend that well? Could he goad your dad into doing something he wouldn't, out of loyalty to a friend? I'd have your back no matter what happened. Would Uncle Chuck do the same for his friend?"

Fear gripped me. What would my dad do in the name of friendship? He and Mr. Feinstein were closer than some brothers I knew. They'd worked together at the landfill for over twenty years. When they retired, both moved to Florida to enjoy the sunshine and cocktails on their lanais together. I glanced across the room. They had joined their wives on the sofa, and each were downing a beer as if nothing unusual had happened tonight.

"Come on. Hank and his officers will solve this mystery. Let's enjoy the rest of the evening and mingle," I said as Porkchop stirred on his pillow at my feet. He and Nina had been quietly snoozing on their pillows in front of the fire. I bent and stroked his head. "You'll have to bring Annie over for a playdate with Porkchop soon. I know he misses her," I said, referring to Candie's dog. She'd become a pup owner a few months ago. While Porkchop was in love with Nina, he was best buds with Annie, a mutt of indeterminate breed Candie had adopted, but I couldn't say the same for Dixie, Candie's calico cat. Dixie and Porkchop tolerated each other.

"I will. Annie would love it," Candie said as we walked over to a group of Loopy Ladies gathered around my dining room table, sampling the food spread out before them.

"Hi, ladies. Anything on your plates that's particularly yummy?" I asked, which was a silly question since rug hookers, after their passion for hooking, loved to party.

Lucy Foster, along with her husband Ralph, owned The Ewe and Me, a rug hooking store. We gathered there every Monday morning to pull loops and gab. She held up her plate piled high with a sample of just about everything people had brought tonight. Her silver bob swept her shoulders as she laughed. "I'll tell you when I'm finished tasting everything on my plate."

"Oh, my," I said. "It all looks so good, I don't know if I could pick a winner."

Cookie Harrington, the youngest member of our group, held up her plate. She was one of Porkchop's favorite people. She worked as the receptionist at the Wings Falls Animal Hospital. After a visit to the hospital for his checkups, she always had a special treat for him. "You have to taste a slice of Franny's banana cream pie. It's to die for."

Heads nodded in agreement all around the table.

My mouth watered thinking about Franny's pie. When Franny moved north over fifteen years ago, she brought her luscious southern-style cooking with her. Her diner was a hit from the first day she flipped over the open sign. I looked across the table where she stood. A smile spread across her face, her white teeth a sharp contrast to her dark skin. She was more than the owner of one of my favorite dining places. She was a good friend, plus Hank's brother dated her niece, Joy. A relationship we were all happy about.

The front door blew open. Cold circled my feet, causing me to shiver. I glanced over to see who had entered my house—Hank and Mark. My heart skipped a beat when I saw Hank. He looked cold and tired. I was about to offer him a hot cup of coffee, but he walked over to my dad and Mr. Feinstein. He didn't make eye contact with me. He spoke in a low voice to them. I knew something was wrong when my mom gasped and a look of terror crossed her face.

CHAPTER TEN

———

Dad and Mr. Feinstein followed Hank out of the house. Dad's usual blustery self was replaced by a man I didn't recognize. A man whose shoulders were slumped and whose usual lively step was replaced with a shuffle as he crossed the room.

I rushed into the living room, followed by Candie. "Mom, what's the matter? Where are Dad and Mr. Feinstein going with Hank?"

Porkchop jumped off his pillow and gazed out the front window at Dad following Hank down my walkway. Porkie's head was bowed, and sadness shone from his chocolate eyes. His usual wagging tail was tucked between his hind legs. What did my loving pup sense was happening?

"Your friend is taking them down to the police station," Mrs. Feinstein said. Her voice shook as if she was about to cry.

I frowned. "The police station? Whatever for?"

Mom brushed back her blonde bangs. "He wants to question them about Theo's death."

I shook my head in disbelief. "Mr. Sayers's death? Why? He was drunk when he left here. He probably tripped and got tangled in that foolish Christmas display of his."

Mark whispered something in Candie's ear. Her eyes widened at whatever he was telling her.

Candie tugged on my arm to get my attention. "Sugar, come into the den. I want to tell you something."

From the tone of her voice, I knew the "something" she wanted to tell me was serious.

Porkchop and I followed her and Mark into the den. My pup and I dropped ourselves onto the loveseat. My heart was practically pounding out of my chest as I glanced around the room. Framed school pictures of me hung on the wall over the desk across the room. They followed my school years from kindergarten to my graduation from college. I glanced at my desk, which was cluttered with computer printouts for the newest children's book I was working on, *More Adventures of Porkchop, the Wonder Dog,* featuring my very own pup. The book would be a follow-up to my first one about Porkchop's adventures. So far, it had been a success. *Right, Porkie?* I thought, running my hand over his sleek fur.

The loveseat cushion next to me sank as Candie sat next to me. She reached over and placed an arm over my shoulder, drawing me close to her. The rhinestones on her sweater pressed into my cheek. Mark stood in front of us, arms folded across his chest.

"Sugar, your daddy and Mr. Feinstein might be in a heap of trouble." Candie glanced up at her husband.

"What are you talking about? Dad's never done anything to warrant being taken to the police station in his life. Let me give Hank a call and see what this is all about." I reached for my phone that I had left on the table next to the sofa before the party had begun and tapped Hank's name.

He answered on the second ring. "Sam, I can't talk right now. I'll give you a call back later." With that, he hung up.

I sat staring at my phone in stunned silence then looked at Candie and Mark. "What's going on? He hung up on me."

Tears rimmed Candie's violet eyes. "Sugar, it looks like Mr. Sayers's death might not have been an accident."

Her words weren't making any sense. Of course, his death was an accident. What else could it be? I jerked in my seat as if struck by lightning. If it wasn't an accident, was Candie saying Mr. Sayers was murdered?

I looked up at Mark then at Candie. "He was murdered? But, by who?" From the solemn looks on Candie's and Mark's faces, it hit me. "No, the police don't think my dad and Mr. Feinstein killed Mr. Sayers. That's ridiculous. After all these years of that jerk harassing my mom and dad, why would Daddy suddenly kill him now? It doesn't make sense." I wanted to scream. Hank didn't know my dad very well. But he certainly knew me. He'd have to know from everything I'd told him about my parents what great people they were. It was all I could do to not jump off the loveseat and drive down to the Wings Falls Police Station and haul my dad and Mr. Feinstein home.

Candie glanced up at Mark, who shifted from one foot to the other. There was something they weren't telling me. "What? What aren't you telling me? Spit it out."

Mark hesitated, studied his hands, and then cleared his throat. "The crime scene guys found prints on the wrappers of the candy canes in your neighbor's mouth."

"So, Mr. Sayers didn't unwrap the candy canes before he stuck them in his mouth," I said. Dread filled me at what Mark had to say next.

He ran a hand over his buzz cut. Mark may not have been tall in stature, matching Candie's five-foot-six, but his heart was as big as a giant's. I knew it pained him to deliver whatever it was he had to say to me. "Yes, the candy canes found in Mr. Sayers's mouth were still wrapped. The tech guys were able to lift a set of prints off them. With today's technology, they were able to process the prints in a matter of minutes."

"That's a good thing, right? The police can go arrest the bad guy."

Mark's next statement dashed any hopes I had. "Ummm, they're your dad's prints."

I swayed in my seat. I wanted to pinch myself to make sure I was awake and this wasn't a nightmare I had fallen into. "Mom? Does my mom know about Dad's prints on the candy canes?"

Mark shook his head. "Hank told your mom and her friend he was taking them down to the station to talk about the argument they had with the victim."

I scooted Porkchop onto the cushion next to me and pushed myself off the loveseat. "I need to go to her." I swayed as I turned to Candie. She grabbed my arms to steady me. "Can you see to the guests? Maybe say something has happened and needs my attention? Should I call Alan Rosenburg? Or would it make my dad and his friend look guilty?" I asked, mentioning our family lawyer.

I walked back into the living room, where the Loopy Ladies and their significant others were enjoying food and drinks, unaware of the nightmare engulfing me. My pup trotted next to me. Mom and Mrs. Feinstein stood by the Christmas tree admiring the ornaments that, only the day before, Hank and I had hung. They acted as if it were an everyday occurrence their husbands took a ride in squad cars to the police station. They turned towards me as I approached them.

"Mom, Mrs. Feinstein, can we talk in the den?" I asked, hating the thought of the conversation I was about to have with them.

Out of the corner of my eye, I noticed Candie approaching my guests and giving them some excuse as to why the party had to end early. Heads nodded as she talked to them. My friends started towards the bedroom, where Hank had stashed their coats. They turned looks of concern towards me as they walked past.

When we were in the den, I closed the door behind us. "Mom, Mrs. Feinstein, please sit." I motioned towards the loveseat I had vacated moments before. I scooped Porkie into my arms for moral support as I dreaded what I was about to tell them.

"Samantha, what is this all about? And what is Candie saying to everyone to end your party so soon? Your father will be disappointed when he and Herb return from the police station if everyone has left. You know how he enjoys a party. I do hope your young man can join us and isn't too busy with the nasty stuff that took place next door."

I mentally shook my head at the innocence of my mom's statement. True, Dad loved a party. Often, he was the life of it, with his sense of humor and giant personality. He was the one who usually pulled a practical joke or more likely was the brunt of one himself. He loved to make people laugh. I only hoped Dad and Mr. Feinstein would be coming home and not spending the night in jail, booked for murder.

CHAPTER ELEVEN

"Mom, what did Hank say to you and Mrs. Feinstein when he took Dad and Mr. Feinstein away with him?" I asked, twisting the hem of my blouse between my fingers.

"Well, of course your Hank heard the guys arguing with Theo. He said he wanted to know more about the disagreement and thought they'd have more privacy down at the station, away from the party, for them to talk. He didn't seem concerned, if that's what you mean," Mom said.

I wrestled with telling Mom and Mrs. Feinstein what Mark had told me. Maybe I was making too much out of it. I was sure there was a perfectly good explanation as to why Dad's prints were on the candy canes. Possibly, Mr. Sayers had dropped them on the way over to his house and Dad picked them up for him. Or Mr. Sayers offered him one, but Dad refused and handed it back. Who knew. There could have been a million reasons his fingerprints were on the candy canes shoved in Mr. Sayers's mouth. I shook my head in frustration. But then, why would Mr. Sayers be sucking on *wrapped* candy canes? None of this made any sense.

I knelt on the floor before my mom and took her hand in mine. I placed Porkchop beside me. He gazed up at Mom, lending me his support. I studied the brown age spots that dotted the back of the slim hand I caressed. When had they appeared? I remembered as a child she'd rub them with lotion as part of her evening ritual. I could almost feel how smooth and soft they were when she'd caress my cheek or brush away my tears if I'd fallen and skinned my knees while playing. When had my mom's hands started to show their age? I looked into her eyes. She may have bleached her hair and styled it differently since I last saw her, but the same love for me I had always known shone forth from her eyes.

"Mom, I think things may be a little more serious than we'd thought earlier tonight."

I hated to see the look of worry that clouded her eyes.

"Sam, what are you talking about? Your dad and Mr. Feinstein are only discussing with Hank the silly argument they had earlier with Mr. Sayers. With all the people milling around, there wasn't any privacy here for Hank to talk to the fellows. Men… Their egos can get so easily bruised. They should have ignored Theo, and he would have gone home."

I hated bursting my mom's bubble of innocence, but she had to know how serious this situation was. "Mom, Mark told me a short time ago that the police found Dad's fingerprints on the wrappers of the candy canes in Mr. Sayers's mouth."

Mrs. Feinstein, who had remained silent until now, gasped. She turned towards my mom and reached out to her with a shaking hand. "Barbara, what is your daughter saying? Do the police think my Herb and your Chuck are involved in that nasty man's death?"

I stood and walked over to the desk across from the loveseat. I didn't want to confirm what she had put into words. To occupy my hands, I reached down and flipped through pages of the picture book manuscript lying on the desk.

"Sam?" my mother asked. Tears laced her words.

I turned and nodded. The pages of my manuscript fluttered in my shaking hands. "Yes, Mom. Dad and Mr. Feinstein might be implicated in my neighbor's death."

Mrs. Feinstein jumped off the loveseat. She stood before me, the picture of rage. Her gray hair bobbled on her shoulders as she jabbed the air with a finger. "It's pure nonsense. My Herb, and I know your father, would never do such a thing." She turned to my mom, who sat with tears streaming down her cheeks. Fear and worry had settled on her shoulders like a heavy shroud. "Barbara, come on. Grab your coat. We're going to drive over to the police station and bust Chuck and Herb out."

In spite of the dire circumstances we now found ourselves in, I had to laugh. I could imagine these avenging angels storming Wings Falls Police Station. Those officers wouldn't know what hit them. "Umm, Mrs. Feinstein, maybe we should calm down a bit and think this through. Mom, do you want to call Alan Rosenburg and see what he has to say about this matter?" Alan had helped me out more than once when I found myself in a legal pickle.

Mom nodded. "That sounds like a good thing to do." She glanced at the digital clock sitting on the edge of the desk. "But it is getting a bit late, and it is Saturday night. He may be out or busy."

"It's worth a try," I said, plucking my phone off the end table. I scrolled through my contact list for his number then tapped his name and listened to the dial tone. I was about to disconnect, thinking Mom was right and he was enjoying his Saturday night, when, "Hello, Sam," came over the line.

"Hi, Alan. I'm sorry to call so late and disturb your evening, but I'm afraid I need your services again."

Alan chuckled. "You're not involved in another murder, are you?"

I cleared my throat. Maybe, with all the murders I'd been involved in, I should put him on a full-time retainer—as if I could afford to. Luckily, he was a family friend and had cut me a break on his fee when I needed him.

"Well, actually, it isn't me this time. It's my dad and his friend."

"How can I help?" All humor had left his voice.

I related to him what had happened tonight. He said he'd be out the door and on his way to the police station in minutes. I thanked him and hung up. I felt like a weight had been lifted off my shoulders, knowing he was now involved.

I related my conversation with Alan to Mom and Mrs. Feinstein. Mrs. Feinstein sank back onto the sofa. I watched as she and Mom embraced. Tears flowed between them. Sometimes having a good friend to lean on in your darkest hours was all you needed.

* * *

"What can I get you ladies this morning? The usual? Grits with a pat of butter on top and a side of bacon for Sam and the ham and eggs special for Candie, right?"

Candie and I sat in our favorite booth in Sweetie Pie's Café, next to the front picture window where we could people watch as we ate our Sunday morning breakfast.

"Joy, you know us too well." I laughed. When had my cousin and I become so predictable? Maybe the next time I stopped in for breakfast, I'd surprise everyone and order one of Franny's ooey gooey cinnamon rolls, which were about the size of a saucer.

"That's right, the usual," I said.

"Me, too," Candie responded as she shifted in her seat.

"Right, got it." Joy jotted down our order then tucked her pen and order pad back into the pocket of the apron that covered the front of her pink uniform. A handkerchief flowed out of the uniform's breast pocket. Joy, who often cooked alongside Aaron in the kitchen, sometimes filled in as waitress when Franny was short-staffed. Franny Goodway had modeled her café after a fifties diner, right down to the waitresses' uniforms. Her café was a happy step back in time, from the black-and-white-checked tile floor to the red vinyl–covered booth seats. I flipped through the tabletop juke box that sat on the end of the booth. Franny's favorites, like mine, were the oldies. I loved Elvis and Roy Orbison. I'd even throw in a few of Donnie Osmond's.

"I'll hand your order in to Aaron and be back in a minute with your coffee. Decaf for you, Sam, right? And pour on the caffeine for you, Candie?"

Everyone at Franny's knew our preferences since we'd been stopping in the café after attending Sunday Mass at Saint Anthony's for over fifteen years when Candie moved north from Hainted Holler, Tennessee—even Joy, who'd only been here for a little over a year.

I let out a soft groan. "Yeah, doctor's orders, decaf for me."

"Got it," Joy said then walked towards the pass-through in the kitchen wall to hand over our order.

Candie laughed then grimaced as I kicked her under the table.

"It's not funny that caffeine raises my blood pressure."

"How's Joy's and Aaron's romance going?" she asked, leaning down to rub her shin.

"Everything's fine from what I know. Hank hasn't said anything to indicate it isn't."

"Speaking of your boyfriend… How were your dad and Mr. Feinstein when they got home from the station last night?" Candie played with the fork set before her.

I shrugged. "Alan drove them home. It was late when they got there. Dad seemed upbeat. I think he's treating this as a big adventure he can take back to Florida with him and tell his buddies. Before I left for Mass this morning, I poked my head in their bedroom and asked if they wanted to join us for breakfast, but Dad mumbled something about being too tired."

"Well, if Uncle Chuck isn't worried, it should be a good thing. Right? Have you heard from Hank?"

"Nope, only a text saying he missed me and would call later." He'd written a few more things, but they were for my eyes only.

"Don't you love your new cell phone? I'm so proud you've come into the twenty-first century."

I stuck my tongue out at Candie. So what if I'd hung onto my flip phone while everyone else was upgrading to the newest and fanciest version of their phone. Big deal.

The bell over the café's door chimed. I glanced over to see who had entered Sweetie Pie's, and my mouth dropped open.

CHAPTER TWELVE

Candie turned in her seat to see what I was staring at. "Is she the officer we saw last night at your neighbor's house? What was her name? Something to do with sleeves?"

I nodded. "Yes, it's Mimi Greensleeves. She certainly looks a lot different out of uniform." From the appreciative glances she was getting from the café 's male customers, I'd say they thought so, too. She was stunning, with her long blonde hair flowing about her shoulders and skinny jeans hugging her slender legs.

She started to walk past our booth, when I called out her name. She stopped and gazed at us. I could tell she was trying to place our faces. Hank had introduced us a few weeks back when I had stopped by the station to visit him.

She flipped her hair over her shoulder and said, "I'm sorry… Your face looks familiar, but I can't recall your name."

"Samantha Davies. I was at the station a few weeks ago, and my boyfriend, Hank Johnson, introduced us. This is my cousin, Candie Parker-Hogan." I pointed across the table.

She shoved her hands into the pockets of the short down parka she was wearing. "Oh, yes. I'm sorry, Samantha. I've met so many people since my husband, Seth, and I moved to Wings Falls. It's nice to meet you, Candie. Any relation to the mayor?"

"Yes, he's my husband," Candie said. A smile spread across her face.

"I've met him once, and he seems like a really nice guy."

Candie puffed up with pride. "The nicest there is," she drawled.

I smiled at the pride in my cousin's voice. Mark was the best mayor Wings Falls has had in many years. "Please call me Sam. My mom's usually the only one who calls me Samantha, and it's when I've done something wrong. Won't you join Candie and me? We ordered our breakfast only a few minutes ago." I patted the bench seat I sat on.

"Thank you. I'd love to. I don't know too many folks yet, except for the officers I work with and they're mainly male. It's nice to talk to a female once in a while." Mimi unzipped her coat, shrugged it off, and hung it on a hook at the end of our booth.

She glanced around the café. It was full of its usual Sunday morning, after church crowd, all enjoying their breakfasts and chatting about the latest goings on in Wings Falls. I wondered if Theo Sayers was the hot topic this morning. "This looks like a very popular café. It's the first time I've been here. Anything in particular you can recommend?"

"Officer, y'all can't go wrong with a stack of Franny's banana or blueberry pancakes. Her cinnamon rolls are to die for, too. Here, take a look and see if there's something to tempt you from the menu." Candie plucked a plastic-coated menu from behind the silver metal napkin holder at the end of the table and handed it to her.

"Thanks, and please call me Mimi," she said then flipped open the menu. "Oh, boy. There's so much to pick from. I don't know if I can choose. Maybe I'd better stick with a bowl of grits. I won't be able to lead anyone through their routines at the gym if I indulge in some of these luscious-looking dishes." She snapped the menu shut and placed it in front of her on the faded red Formica tabletop. She lifted a slim hand to her mouth and tried to stifle a yawn.

"I'm sorry. Believe me, it's not the company. I didn't get home until late last night," Mimi said, looking slightly embarrassed.

This was a perfect opportunity for me to ask her if she knew anything about Mr. Sayers's death without looking too obvious. "I saw you at the Sayers's residence. I noticed you didn't finish until late. It was an unfortunate accident."

Mimi raised one of her well-shaped blonde eyebrows at me. "You knew the victim?"

Okay, I needed to sound casual about this if I was going to get any info out of her. "Yes. He was my neighbor. It's such a tragedy he got tangled in his Christmas display. He put so much love and work into it. He planned all year for the holiday season and took such pride in his yearly display. He wanted to bring joy and a bit of fun to the neighborhood."

Candie nudged my foot under the table. I didn't dare look at her for fear I'd burst out laughing. Okay, so I was laying it on a bit thick for Officer Greensleeves.

Mimi tapped her fingers on the menu. "I can't say much about the investigation. I spent most of my time talking to his wife." She turned to me. "Mrs. Sayers mentioned that right before she went outside to check on her husband, she heard a car backfire then screech down the street. Did you see or hear anything?"

This was the first time I'd heard of a car speeding down my street. "No, I'm afraid I didn't. I had a party going on in my house, so there was a lot of chatter to drown out any outside noise."

Mimi nodded, and I had the feeling this conversation had ended.

Joy stopped by our table with two coffee pots and an extra white porcelain mug. She placed the mug in front of Mimi. "Coffee?" she asked, holding up the pots.

Mimi nodded. "Yes. Please. I need lots of caffeine this morning."

We all laughed as Joy filled Mimi's plus Candie's and my mugs with our coffee of choice.

The bell over the door chimed again. I looked over to see Joe Peters limp into the café. I nodded towards him and asked, "I wonder what happened to Joe? Last night I noticed he was limping."

Mimi sipped her coffee then grimaced. "I'm afraid it's my fault."

Candie and I gave her a questioning look. "What did you do? Tackle him?" Candie asked with a laugh.

"As I'm sure you realize, with Seth's job as a fireman and mine as a police officer, we both work shifts, and they often don't coincide. To fill the long hours at home, I've taken a job at Fitness World as a personal trainer." Mimi stirred a dollop of cream into her coffee.

My eyebrows rose at this information. I couldn't see Joe Peters working out at the gym, at least not voluntarily. "Don't tell me Joe is a member of the gym?"

Mimi took a swallow of her coffee then placed the mug on the table in front of her. "The station commander has enacted an old requirement of the Wings Falls Police force. One that has a few guys at the station grumbling."

"What is it?" Candie asked, tapping her ruby red fingernail on the tabletop.

Mimi wrapped her hands around her coffee mug. "Apparently, one of the terms of employment states no officer may be more than twenty pounds overweight."

I choked on the mouthful of coffee I had sipped. I grabbed a napkin out of the metal holder so I didn't sputter it down the front of my fleece top. A giggle bubbled up inside of me. I couldn't help it. Joe Peters had a long way to go to meet the force's weight guideline. The buttons on his uniform shirts strained to the point of almost popping off.

He walked towards us on the way to a table. "Hi Joe," I said then looked him up and down. "I guess your usual three-doughnut breakfast is off the menu today."

His unibrow furrowed at my comment. He grumbled something unintelligible at me, which, if I interpreted it correctly, had something to do with putting my coffee mug someplace where the sun didn't shine.

I opened my mouth to reply, but Candie swatted my arm. "Sam, don't let the man jerk your tail. He ain't worth spit after all he's put you through."

Mimi sent me a quizzical look over the rim of her coffee mug. It was no secret Joe and I had a history, so I thought I'd bring her up to date on our relationship. She'd find out about it soon enough at the police station. If my name ever came up in a conversation, I was sure Joe would gladly give Mimi his version of me, and it wouldn't be flattering.

I nodded towards Joe's retreating back. "I've known Joe since we were in kindergarten together." I related what had happened all those years ago and how Joe had held a grudge against me ever since.

"You mean to say he has accused you of murder?" Mimi asked incredulously.

"He'd love to lock me up and throw away the key."

"Hmm, maybe I see a few more squats and an extra lap or two around the gym in his future," Mimi said, tapping her finger against the side of her head.

Candie and I laughed. Wouldn't it be sweet revenge, and he'd never know his added workout was because of what I'd told Mimi...

A phone buzzed, and Mimi reached inside her jeans pocket to retrieve hers. She swiped the front and listened intently to the conversation on the other end. She said, "Okay," a few times then disconnected. She stared across the table at Candie and me. A chill shot through me as her cool blue eyes focused on my face.

"Ladies, I'm afraid I have to return to the station. Please tell the waitress I'm sorry I can't stay for one of the café's delicious breakfasts. It's been nice talking to you two." Mimi grabbed her wallet out of her purse, dug out a five-dollar bill, and placed it on the table. She slid out of the booth, grabbed her coat, and hurried out of the café. A minute later, a limping Joe Peters followed her out of the restaurant. The bell over the door jingled in their wake. Their cars sped out of the parking lot in the direction of the police station.

"Well, I declare… Mimi and Joe both left as if their tails were on fire," Candie said, squinting towards the café's door. One of these days she'd admit she needed glasses.

"Yes, I wonder what it's all about," I said, frowning. Now, Elvis's "Hound Dog" echoed from the depths of my Gucci handbag.

CHAPTER THIRTEEN

———

Mom's name flashed across my caller ID. I swiped my phone then held it up to my ear. "Mom, what's up?"

A sobbing voice met my question. My heart started to race in my chest. Had something drastic happened to my parents? Did Dad have a heart attack? My imagination was working in overdrive.

"Mom? Mom, please, I can't understand what you are saying. Did something happen to Dad? Are *you* all right? What? Hank called and asked Dad to stop by police the station again? I'll be right home."

"What's happened?" Candie asked, looking up from stirring more sugar into her coffee. Her sweet tooth was as bad as mine. "Why does Uncle Chuck have to go to the police station? I thought everything was settled last night when he went there to answer Hank's questions."

I shrugged. "I don't know. I thought so, too, but it seems Hank has a few more questions for him. I wonder if I should call his lawyer and let him know the latest development, but maybe doing so would make it look as if Dad has something to hide… What do you think?"

"It's up to y'all, but I don't think it would hurt. It can't be too serious if the police didn't send a squad car to pick up your dad." Candie grinned. "I can imagine the stories Uncle Chuck will tell his buddies once he returns to Florida. Wait. How is he going to get there? They don't have a car at their disposal."

"Dad called Gladys, and she said he could borrow her car while they're in town. She said her Pookie Bear could take her wherever she needed to go." I could just imagine my dad driving my neighbor Gladys's hot pink Chevy Chevelle SS. She called it her "love machine." I didn't know why she'd given it a nickname, nor did I want to. That was TMI as far as I was concerned. She'd had it custom painted pink and covered the seats with fuzzy pink leopard print slip covers. The steering wheel was wrapped in matching pink leopard.

Candie laughed. "I can just see Uncle Chuck behind the wheel, but that's Gladys for you, ever ready to help. I'm sure she wants first dibs on any gossip concerning Mr. Sayers's death."

"That will be a small price to pay for the use of her car." I glanced around the room for Joy. I wanted to pay for my meal and coffee, even though I hadn't been able to enjoy it. I spied her across the café. She was busy with another customer delivering their order. "Can you please tell Joy I'm sorry I couldn't stay? I need to get home and see to Mom. Maybe I can call Hank and see what is happening." I reached into my purse and pulled out my wallet. I plucked out the amount I knew my breakfast would cost plus a tip and laid the money on the table next to my coffee mug.

"You're not going to leave me out of this drama. I'm coming with you," Candie said, searching her lavender-spangled purse for her wallet.

I shook my head. "Candie, you don't have to do that. I'm sure Mark will want to spend the rest of the afternoon with you, not to mention Dixie and Annie."

"Oh, pooh." Candie waved bejeweled fingers at me. "I wouldn't have seen much of him today, anyway. He's going to be walled up in the den this afternoon working on a speech he has to give next week to the city council about improvements he wants to make to the town's sewage system. He'll love the company of our two fur babies. Let me call and tell him my change of plans." She reached into her purse again and pulled out her blinged-out phone. I smiled at all the sparkle my cousin radiated.

As she talked to her hubby, I slid out of our booth and crossed the café to Joy. "Joy, I'm afraid Candie and I have to leave. We've left the money for our breakfasts on the table." I pointed towards our booth.

Joy turned towards me. A frown creased her forehead. "Oh, my. I hope there isn't anything wrong. You don't have to pay for the meals."

"Don't be silly. Of course we do. Surprise a random customer with our breakfasts." Since she'd started dating Hank's brother, Aaron, Joy and I had become good friends. I felt comfortable confiding in her the reason I had to leave so abruptly.

"My mother called. She's in a state because my dad was asked to go back to the police station to answer more questions about last night."

Joy glanced around the room and then, in a voice barely above a whisper, said, "It was tragic what happened to your neighbor. He'd stop in here once in a while, always alone. The last time was earlier this week. In fact, he sat in the booth where you and Candie are sitting. He was acting really strange, though."

Joy's last sentence had caught my attention. "Strange? Like how?"

"He kept staring out the window as if he was looking for someone, and when I asked him if he wanted any coffee, he about jumped a foot off his seat."

Now my interest was really piqued. Who could Mr. Sayers have been looking for, and why was he so nervous? "Did anyone ever join him in his booth?"

Joy's tightly curled ponytail swung back and forth as she shook her head. "That's the strange thing. I heard a car backfire outside, and then he got up and ran out of the café. He nearly knocked over a couple on his way out. Didn't even apologize to them."

I mulled Joy's information over and frowned. "He always was an odd duck. Who knows what he was up to?" I gave Joy a side hug then returned to my table.

Candie had already donned her coat. I snatched mine off the hook and slid my arms into the sleeves. After I'd zipped it up, I reached into the booth for my purse. "Ready?" I asked.

Candie nodded in reply. On the way out to the parking lot and our cars, I relayed to her what Joy had said about Mr. Sayers.

"Hmm, it does seem odd. Who do you think he was watching for? And why didn't he meet them in the restaurant instead of running outside?" my cousin asked as she opened the door to Precious, her baby blue '73 Mustang.

I dug in my coat pocket for the keys to my egg-yolk-yellow VW Bug. I had parked next to her car. "It sure does. I wonder what made him so jittery? Come on. We'd better get to my house and see how my mom is," I said, sliding into my car.

Candie nodded. "That varmint was probably up to no good. Why else would he have been so on edge?" She slipped into her car and placed the key in the ignition.

It was less than a ten-minute drive from Sweetie Pie's to my house. As I entered the front door, my heart broke at the sight of my mom huddled on the sofa with tears streaming down her face. Porkchop sat curled up on her lap, lending her his warmth and comfort.

I tossed my purse on the trunk in front of the sofa then sat down next to her. I reached over and pulled her into my arms. Porkchop came with her. It hit me how often when I was growing up, I'd sat on this very sofa and Mom would cradle me in her arms and wipe away my tears. I caught the twinkling lights of my Christmas tree out of the corner of my eye. What a difference a day—or even a few hours—could make. Last night my family and friends enjoyed each other's company in my home, and today my dad was involved in a murder investigation.

"I'll go into the kitchen and brew up some tea," Candie said, taking off her coat and laying it on the wing chair by the fireplace.

"Mom, what exactly did Hank say to Dad?"

Porkchop lifted his head at the sound of my voice. He gave me a wag of his tail but remained on my mom's lap. I believe he sensed that right now she needed the comfort of his warm body more than he needed a scratchie from me.

Mom hiccupped and swiped a tissue across her eyes. "He said he wanted to ask your father about the time when he worked at the landfill."

"Landfill?" I asked. "What would where he worked have to do with Mr. Sayers's murder?"

Mom shrugged. "I don't know, sweetheart. Your father has been retired from there for over five years now."

"I'm going to call Hank and see if I can find something out." I reached over for my purse and pulled out my phone then hit his number.

He answered on the second ring. "Hi, Sam. Your dad is doing fine. I had a couple of questions about when he worked for the landfill. He should be home shortly."

I laughed. "I guess you knew why I was calling without me even asking?"

"You mean you didn't call me for that reason?"

I could hear the smile in his voice. He knew me too well.

There was no need to beat around the bush since he already knew why I had called. "Okay, so why did my dad have to go back to the police station? Didn't he tell you everything you needed to know last night?"

"Umm," Hank said. He was hesitant to answer any question I might have. "Let's just say we've gone through your neighbor's laptop, and it had a lot of very interesting information on it."

"You're not going to tell me what you found on the laptop, are you?" My voice had a whining tone to it.

"No, I'm not, and I don't want you to stick your pretty little nose into this investigation, either."

I silently groaned. It wasn't the first—or even the third—time I'd heard this admonition from Hank. But we were talking about my dad who was in trouble. I needed to help.

A deep sigh traveled over the phone. "Sam, you know I can't. It is part of a murder investigation."

A frustrated sigh escaped me as well. "All right. I'll let you go. You said my dad is on his way home?"

"Yes, he left right before you called. I like him, Sam. He's quite a character. I can see where you get your spunk from."

I chuckled. "Yep. They broke the mold when Dad was born. I'll take it as a compliment when you compare me to him. Will I see you tonight?"

"I'm not sure. I hope so. You know how my schedule is when I'm involved in a murder investigation."

Yeah, I did. Our alone time was severely limited, but such was life when dating a police officer. "Okay. You have a key to the front door."

"I love you, Sam."

"Love you, too," I answered back, wishing I could say it to him in person.

"Your father's on his way home?" My mom blinked back fresh tears. "What else did Hank say?"

"Here you go, Aunt Barbara. No cream but three sugars, right?" I hadn't heard Candie come into the living room with Mom's tea. She stood next to the sofa holding a Harry Potter mug with steam overflowing the rim.

Mom reached up for the offered mug. "Thank you, dear. I can't believe you remembered how I take my tea. It's so thoughtful of you."

"Of course I'd remember how my favorite aunt loves her tea," Candie said, handing the mug over to Mom.

I laughed. "She's your only aunt." Candie and I were both only children, so our extended family was very limited.

I glanced around the living room, taking in the Christmas tree and all the holiday decorations Hank and I had placed around the room. A ceramic Mr. and Mrs. Claus sat on the table next to the sofa. A group of Santa's elves lined the mantel over the fireplace. I remembered these decorations from my childhood.

The front door banged open, and this time, Porkchop did jump off the sofa and race to greet the newcomer.

CHAPTER FOURTEEN

―――――

"Well, looky here. The prettiest ladies in all of Wing Falls are gathered in my living room."

"Dad," I said, rising from the sofa, but Mom beat me to him. She flung her arms around his thick neck.

As he walked farther into the living room, his arm around Mom, he unbuttoned his corduroy cargo coat and flung it over the back of the sofa. He'd replaced his shorts with a pair of jeans. I smiled at his sweatshirt. I wondered what Hank thought of the saying, *Lovers Do it Better in Florida,* written across the front.

"What did Hank ask you at the police station?" I asked, hoping I could guess where his investigation was going.

Dad frowned. "Well, he wasn't the only one asking questions. There was that snot-nosed kid you went to school with. What was his name? Jim, John, Joe? Joe, that's it. He had a real chip on his shoulder."

I groaned. "Joe Peters." I glanced at Candie. "So that's where he rushed off to when he left Sweetie Pie's."

Candie nodded. "I imagine that's where Mimi went, too."

"If you mean a young blonde lady officer, she was there, but she sat quiet mostly, typing into a computer thingy."

I had to laugh. If I thought I was techno-challenged, my dad was a dinosaur. "So, what did Joe and Hank ask you?" I was itching to hear where the questioning had led.

"They asked about my working at the landfill. It was kind of strange, though."

I was becoming frustrated. Pulling teeth would have been easier than getting answers out of my dad. "How was it strange?"

Dad plopped onto the sofa. Porkchop immediately jumped up and curled onto his lap. "They asked about how the landfill is run, the fellow who owns it, and the Ferguson Construction Company."

"The Ferguson Construction Company? Aren't they the ones who built this house back in the fifties?" Mom asked.

When she snuggled up next to Dad and Porkchop, I sat in one of the wing chairs next to the fireplace. Candie got comfortable in the other.

"Yep, they've been around for years. The father of the fellow in charge now started the company after he got out of the Army when World War II ended."

"Oh, I know the younger Mr. Ferguson. He's always stopping by city hall applying for building permits," Candie said. Since she was Mark's secretary, she was privy to this information. "I heard the father will be retiring soon, something to do with his health, and his son will take over the reins of the company."

"Wow, a third-generation company. That's nice to see," Mom said then took a sip of her tea.

"Why do you think the police want to know about them? What would they have to do with Theo?" Mom asked, frowning over the rim of the mug.

Dad shrugged. "Darn if I know. I really never had much contact with Mr. Ferguson and his son. I only dealt with the drivers of their trucks when they came to the landfill."

An idea flashed through my brain. I looked over to Candie. "You know people left a lot of their goodies behind last night. Care to visit the widow Sayers with an offering and give her our condolences?"

She shot me a questioning look, and then a light appeared to click on in her violet eyes. "Certainly. It's the neighborly thing to do. Memaw Parker would be so proud of us. You know how important good manners were to her."

My mom looked from Candie to me. "Sam, what are you up to? I don't want you getting involved in Theo's murder. And don't use your grandmother as an excuse to meddle."

"What, me stick my nose where it doesn't belong? Mom, you know me better than that," I said.

Mom chuckled. "That's it. I know you too well. Whatever you do, please be careful. Your father and I can handle everything the police have to say about Mr. Sayers's death. I know your dad is innocent." Mom reached up and kissed Dad on his suntanned cheek.

"I believe I saw a plate of brownies on the counter in the kitchen," Candie said, rising from her chair. She smoothed down her gauzy skirt and tucked a strand of auburn hair behind her ear.

My curly ponytail bobbed up and down as I nodded. "Yes, Helen brought those. They'd be the perfect goodie to take to the grieving widow." I stood and walked into the kitchen with my cousin.

* * *

"It's cold enough to freeze the you-know-what off a brass monkey," Candie said, stomping her feet on the top wooden step of the Sayers's front porch.

I smiled. My dear Southern cousin had a colorful way of phrasing things. It must be the reason the romance novels she wrote in her spare time were such a hit, but I had to agree with her. The temperature had to register below freezing. The plate of brownies I clutched in my mittened hands shook as I shivered.

"Yeah, I hope Mrs. Sayers answers the door soon, or I'll be an icicle. Oh, I think I see her coming," I said, spying a shadow approaching us through the glass insert in the front door.

The door opened to a reveal a tiny slip of a woman who appeared to be about my mom's age. She wore a faded green robe wrapped around her slim body and clutched the collar in her hands at her neck. Her gray hair hung in matted strands about her face. I glanced down and saw her feet were bare of slippers. I shivered at the thought of them on the cold tile floor of her entryway.

Because of the rivalry between my dad and Mr. Sayers, our families had never been close. I'd see Mrs. Sayers from a distance tending her gardens in the summer, but once fall and colder weather set in, she seldom set foot into her yard. They never had any children, so there wasn't any reason for me to visit them. She seemed pleasant enough, unlike her husband, waving to me from her car if he was driving her somewhere. In fact, I wondered if she even knew how to drive, as I'd never seen her behind the wheel of their car. Now Mr. Sayers, he was a horse of a different color, as Memaw Parker would say. The only contact my parents had with him was when Dad and Mr. Sayers were shouting at each other from their respective yards over some slight one perceived the other had made, like our leaves blowing into their yard or some such silly thing. Even as a child, I'd shake my head at their foolishness.

"Can I help you ladies?" Mrs. Sayers asked in a small, nervous voice. It was obvious from the frown on her face that she didn't know who we were.

"Mrs. Sayers, I'm Samantha Davies."

She looked at me with dull brown eyes. She raised a shaking hand to smooth back her hair.

I nodded in the direction of my house. "I live next door, and this is my cousin, Candie Parker-Hogan. We heard of your husband's unfortunate accident and brought you a little something as an expression of our sympathy." I held out the plate of brownies to her.

Her mouth formed an *O* as she reached for the plate. "Oh, my. This is so thoughtful of you two. Thank you so much." She stepped back to close the door.

Before she closed it in our faces, I asked, "Would you like some company? Can Candie and I do anything for you?"

Mrs. Sayers's looked from me to Candie then glanced down the street. Why was she so nervous? Was she expecting someone— maybe the police? Was she on edge because she had killed her husband?

CHAPTER FIFTEEN

Candie spoke up. "How about I fix you a cup of tea to go with those delicious brownies? I'm sure after the terrible events of last night, you could use a bit of company?"

I smiled. Candie was going to get us into Mrs. Sayers's home whether the woman wanted us there or not.

"Well, all right. I guess I'm not being very hospitable. You see, Theo never allowed me to entertain. He didn't like having people in our home."

I knew he wasn't a social butterfly, but to inflict such a solitary life on his wife? I wondered if she'd had enough and snapped.

We followed her into the living room. It had a cozy but slightly dated feel to it. A green corduroy recliner sat next to the fireplace. A matching lavender chintz recliner took up residence on the opposite side of the fireplace with a basket overflowing with yarn on the floor next to it. Knitting needles poked out of the basket. What looked like a project in progress lay on the cushion of the chair. A gigantic flat screen television hung on the wall opposite the chairs. A loveseat was positioned under it.

"The kitchen is through the dining room. The kettle is already on the stove, and the cups and tea bags are in the cabinet next to the sink," Mrs. Sayers said, pointing towards the kitchen.

I turned to Candie, and she nodded. I could have clapped my hands with glee at this golden opportunity to quiz Mrs. Sayers. "Your home is laid out like mine. I guess we had the same builder."

Mrs. Sayers nodded as she placed the brownies on the coffee table in front of the loveseat. "Yes, I believe so. In fact, I believe the Ferguson Construction Company built most of the homes on our street."

I claimed the loveseat. Mrs. Sayers crossed over to the recliner, removed the knitting project from the seat, and sat. Candie went into the kitchen to make the tea while Mrs. Sayers and I exchanged small talk. I didn't want to get into anything concerning Mr. Sayers until my cousin was back to support me.

In less than ten minutes, I heard the tea kettle whistling. Candie returned to the living room with a tray filled with rose-patterned china teacups and plates, a matching sugar bowl and creamer, and a stack of paper napkins. She placed the tray on the table next to the brownies. What looked like sterling silver spoons lay next to the dessert plates on the tray.

"Mrs. Sayers, this is beautiful china and silver." I flicked my hand towards the tray.

"Please, call me Rosa. Mrs. Sayers makes me sound so old. Yes, they belonged to my mother."

"I saw them on the hutch in your kitchen. I hope you don't mind that I used them for our tea and brownies. Tea always tastes so much better when served in fine china," Candie said, sitting on the loveseat next to me.

"I agree," Rosa said. She rose from the recliner, poured herself a cup of tea, placed a brownie on a plate, and then returned to her seat.

"Rosa, I know we've lived next door to each other for years, but I'm sorry to say we've never gotten to know each other. Now that your husband is gone, I hope you'll call on me if you need anything." I picked up a brownie and placed it on one of the china plates. I was used to paper plates and hoped I didn't drop and break her beautiful dinnerware.

Rosa took a sip of her tea then frowned. "I'm afraid the silly feud between Theo and your dad prevented us from getting to know each other, but I would like to now."

I nodded. "My parents didn't speak about it much, so I only know a wee bit of what caused it. I guess your husband had a crush on Mom years ago and was upset when she didn't return his affections." Okay, so I knew the whole story, or at least I thought I did, but I wanted Rosa to tell me what she knew about Mr. Sayers's unrequited love.

Mrs. Sayers frowned. "*Humph.* Theo was a fool when it came to your mom. He had a blind spot about her, and I was an even bigger fool thinking that I could change him."

Candie and I sat up straighter in our seats. Did I see a determined look in Rosa's eyes, as if now that Theo was dead, nothing was going to hold her back? What did Rosa mean by what she had said? Was all not love and kisses in the Sayers's household?

"I tried. Heaven knows how I tried to win over Theo's heart, but to no avail. It was always Barbara this and Barbara that. When you were born, that was the topper. We had wanted to have children, but God didn't bless us. Theo thought I was less of a woman after you were born." Rosa shook her head, as if trying to dispel all those feelings weighing her down from years of abuse by her husband.

My heart squeezed in my chest for Rosa. My marriage may have ended in a disaster, but at least George never abused me, mentally or physically. "Rosa, I'm so sorry you had to live like this all these years."

Candie rose from the loveseat and walked over to Rosa. She knelt and took Rosa's hand into hers. "Sugar, I'm sure you are more woman than he ever deserved."

I nodded in agreement. "Rosa, I wish my mom knew about this years ago. She would have been a great friend to you."

Candie returned to the loveseat and took a sip of her tea and a bite of brownie.

"Theo would never have allowed me to befriend your mom. At times, I felt like a prisoner in my own home. My only outlet was my knitting." She reached into the basket next to her chair, pulled out her knitting project, and held it up for us to see. "I knit hats for preemie babies and donate them to local hospitals."

"How sweet," I said, admiring the tiny knitted hat that couldn't be bigger than the size of my fist.

"Rosa, who do you think killed your husband? Did he have any disagreements with anyone lately?" Candie asked then dabbed at her lips for any stray brownie crumbs.

My head swiveled around to her. I guess there was nothing like getting to the point of our visit.

Rosa frowned. "There weren't too many people he did get along with. You know he was still working for the *Tribune*?"

I reached over and snatched another brownie off the plate. They were delicious, and I couldn't stop at one. "I had heard something about his working part-time as an investigative reporter. Was he writing an article that upset someone?"

"Upset someone?" Rosa let out a dry chuckle. "That was Theo's main aim in life—to rattle people's cages. He wouldn't be happy if he wasn't causing a commotion. I think that was the only thing that made him happy. It certainly wasn't me."

I gave a side-glance to Candie at Rosa's last statement. Was she so unhappy in her marriage that she'd had enough and killed her husband? When I'd been involved in past murder investigations, Candie had told me to look at the person who was closest to the victim to find the culprit. Maybe this was the case in Mr. Sayers's murder.

Candie swallowed a bite of brownie then asked, "So, was he working on an article that 'rattled someone's cage,' as you said?"

"All I know is that he started to get phone calls where he'd wind up in a heated argument with whoever was on the other end of the line. I'd ask Theo who had called, but he'd only say it was a wrong number or a telemarketer," Rosa said, fingering the tiny baby's hat.

"Did you tell the police this?" I asked, flicking brownie crumbs off the front of my sweater and onto a napkin.

Rosa's eyes rounded. "Do you think I should? I didn't feel the calls were important yesterday when they were here. Like I said, I figured they were telemarketers or some such thing. Those really got under Theo's skin."

I had the feeling they were more than spam calls. Even though we all thought those calls were irritating, especially when they came at an inconvenient time like when you were in the shower, were they enough to get angry over? I didn't think so. Who could have been calling him? Was it the murderer?

"Rosa, do you know anything about the latest article he was working on? Could his phone calls have been related to it?" If I wanted to make sure Dad and Mr. Feinstein weren't implicated in Mr. Sayers's death, I had to start asking some hard questions.

Rosa tapped the side of her head with a finger. "Now that you mention it, that young reporter from the *Tribune,* what's his name… Rob something or other? I'm sorry my old brain isn't what it used to be. Well, he came by yesterday afternoon."

I jerked up in my seat and turned to Candie. I'd bet Porkchop's next bag of kibble that it was Rob Anderson. A sneaky reporter who thought he was going to be the next Pulitzer Prize winner. He'd caused more than his fair share of trouble in Candie's life last summer when he tried to implicate my cousin in a murder right before her wedding. He printed a risqué picture of her and her first fiancé on the front page of the *Tribune.* It had caused quite a stir in Wings Falls, especially with Mark running for reelection as mayor, too.

"Rosa, was his last name Anderson by any chance? A skinny fellow with longish brown hair, a pockmarked face, scuffed brown shoes, and baggy jeans?" I'd never seen him wear anything other than those shoes and jeans, so I had a hunch that if the Rob she was referring to was wearing this outfit, it was Rob Anderson.

Rosa clapped her hands in excitement. "That's him. I showed him into our den where Theo was working and left them alone. I came back here to do my knitting. Anyway, they got into quite an argument. Next thing I knew, Theo was showing him to the front door and none too gently either. This Rob said something to Theo about how he'd be sorry, and he'd have his job sooner than later."

My jaw dropped open at what Rosa had described. Could Rob have returned later in the evening and killed Mr. Sayers, or was Mrs. Sayers eager to pin the murder on someone other than herself?

CHAPTER SIXTEEN

———

Candie and I visited with Rosa for about a half an hour, and then Candie made the excuse she had to get home to her hubby and fur babies. As Rosa walked us to the door, I noticed a beautiful bouquet of red roses on a table in the entryway that I'd missed on the way into her home. I must have been too absorbed into getting my foot in the door.

"Rosa, what beautiful flowers, and at this time of year," I said, leaning over and giving them a sniff.

"Umm, yes. Well, a friend heard of Theo's passing and sent them to me," Rosa said, twisting the ends of a strand of hair in her fingers.

"Thank you for your time, and we won't bother you anymore," I said, opening the door and stepping outside.

With the door closed behind us, I shook my head and said, "I thought she said she didn't have any friends."

"Take a look at this." Candie handed me a small white card with the name of a local florist printed on the back.

Years may have passed, but now it's time for you and me.

My eyes widened as I looked at Candie. "Where did this come from?"

A smile lifted the corners of Candie's mouth. "It kind of slipped into the palm of my hand while you were talking with Rosa."

Again, I thought, could Rosa have killed her husband to be free of him?

I looked at Candie. "Maybe she had a flame from years ago who she wanted to get back with, but she had to get rid of Theo first?"

Candie nodded.

* * *

The bell over the door to The Ewe and Me jingled as I pushed my way into the wool shop where my rug hooking group, the Loopy Ladies, met on Monday mornings.

With Mom and Dad in town, I was going to pass on today's meeting, but since they had the use of Gladys's car, Mom encouraged me to go, as she and Dad had some last-minute Christmas shopping and I shouldn't expect them home until later this afternoon. They also wanted to catch up with friends they hadn't seen since their trip north last year.

I plunked my gear—which consisted of a red canvas bag filled with my hooking frame, pattern, wool, hook, and scissors—onto the long wooden table where fellow hookers were gathered. I unclipped Porkchop's leash. He usually accompanied me to The Ewe on Mondays. He scooched under the table and settled onto the doggie bed Lucy had placed there for his use. Porkchop fancied himself the official shop dog. Other hookers would sometimes bring their own pets—like Patsy Ikeda, who would often bring her Japanese Spitz, Hana—but Porkchop acted as if he was the top dog. I took my usual seat next to Candie. She had arrived before me and was already pulling loops through a pattern featuring a calico cat, reminiscent of her Dixie, curled up on a rug. I was happy to see everyone, even though we'd been together on Saturday night at my house. The Ewe was a home away from home for us hookers. I glanced around the room where we'd hook and, yes, gossip. The walls were lined with cubbies and antique dressers overflowing with wool for our projects. My favorite wools were hand-dyed by Lucy. There was a room off this main one where Lucy worked her magic over her porcelain dye pots. Occasionally, she'd let us join in and brew up a color of our own.

"So tell me, Sam… Has Hank found out who Theo's killer is yet? I'm telling you it's not safe anywhere nowadays. Why, I told my Pookie Bear to get out his old baseball bat and place it next to our bed. A person could sneak into your house and try to murder you in the middle of the night."

While Mr. Sayers's murder was a serious matter, I had to smile at Gladys's comment. I could picture her thin-as-a-rail boyfriend whacking an intruder, and Gladys wasn't much bigger than him.

"What's become of our beloved town?" Helen asked. Her wardrobe choice today was a bright-orange flowered top she'd paired with red polyester pants. "I remember when Wings Falls was named Hometown USA by a national magazine." For once, Helen and Gladys were in agreement on something. That didn't happen very often.

Twelve heads nodded around the table. All the members of the group were here today. I was sure my neighbor's murder was part of the reason everyone was present. A little gossip was a great incentive to gather.

"Has Hank mentioned anything about the murder? I hate to go out in our backyard with my kids to play, knowing there's a killer walking around Wings Falls," Susan Mayfield said, looking up from her project of colorful Easter eggs.

Heads nodded around the table once more as the ladies pulled loops of wool through their patterns. "Anyone care for a cup of coffee?"

We all swiveled in our seats towards the direction of the voice. Lucy, the co-owner of The Ewe, pushed a metal cart in from the back room. It was laden with paper cups, plates, and a pot of coffee. Next to the coffee sat an open box filled with cinnamon buns. My mouth watered in anticipation of eating one.

"Did Ralph make an early run to Sweetie Pie's?" I asked, recognizing the Danish as Franny Goodway's. Ralph was Lucy's husband, The Ewe's other owner. He was also responsible for supplying Porkchop with treats while we visited.

Lucy's gray hair, styled into a bob, swung about her shoulders as she nodded. "I think he arrived there right when the café opened so he'd be able to buy enough for you ladies before they sold out."

Sweetie Pie's cinnamon buns were a Wings Falls' favorite. A person had to be at the café when it opened to be guaranteed one of these delights. Latecomers would be disappointed.

As we enjoyed our goodies and coffee, the conversation returned to Mr. Sayers's murder.

"Sam, you're his neighbor. Who do you think killed Theo?" Jane Burrows, our town's librarian, asked. She tugged at the front of the festive red sweater set she wore. Sweater sets and khaki slacks were her daily wardrobe.

I shrugged. "I have no idea. My family and I may have lived next to them, but we had very little interaction with the Sayers." I was keeping Candie's and my suspicions about Rob Anderson and Rosa Sayers to myself.

"I'll tell you who felt like throttling him… My husband Tony."

My eyes jerked to the end of the table where Anita Plum sat jabbing the air with her rug hook. Anita taught at the Wings Falls High School as a substitute, which gave her time to join us when she wasn't called in to teach.

We all sat waiting for her to elaborate on what her bold statement meant. "Why do you say that?" I asked as I stretched my pattern over my frame.

Anita laid her hook on the table and took a sip of her coffee. It was all I could do not to waggle my fingers at her to hurry up. "You know my twins."

We all nodded. Anita had twin teenage girls, Susie and Sara, who kept her hopping with their antics and ever-changing hormones. While they caused Anita another gray hair, their escapades were the cause for a lot of laughter when Anita related their stories to the Loopy Ladies.

"They have a job at the mall over the holiday season as Santa's helper, taking pictures of the kids as they sit on Santa's lap," Anita said.

"So, what does that have to do with Theo?" Helen asked, an impatient tone in her voice.

I wanted to stuff a piece of wool in Helen's mouth so Anita would continue her story. "I heard he was one of the mall's Santas. Did he get fresh with your girls?" I asked. I dreaded the answer she'd give me.

"He didn't touch them or anything like that, but every once in a while, he'd tell them an off-color joke. It really made them uncomfortable. I told the girls to quit, but they said they weren't going to let a dirty old Santa drive them away from their job. You know how stubborn teenagers can be. They liked what they were doing and loved dealing with the kids. My Susie wants to go to college and take photojournalism. She loves the experience she's getting snapping pictures of the kids. And Sara wants to be a preschool teacher. She really enjoys talking to the young kids as they visit Santa."

"So, I take it Tony was pretty upset with this Santa," Candie asked, adding an orange loop to her cat's paw.

"Oh, he was in real Papa Bear mode when he found out what Theo was doing. He went right to the mall's management office to complain and demanded they fire him," Anita said.

"That was a smart move on his part," I said. Certainly, smarter than marching into the mall and punching Mr. Sayers out. Something I feared my own father would have done. In his eyes, you didn't mess with the Reynolds' women.

"Thankfully, he thought first before acting on his emotions, but the mall manager hinted that he was about to fire Theo anyway." Anita laid her hook on top of her project. She had everyone's attention.

"How come?" Gladys asked. Cinnamon bun crumbs rested on the front of her sweater, dusting a grinning Santa face.

"Apparently, Theo had made uncalled-for comments to some of the moms, too. One of them was threatening to sue the mall. From what I've heard, the mall is in financial trouble and couldn't afford a lawsuit," Anita said.

Groans and *ewws* circled the table. It looked as if no one wanted the picture of Theo being nasty to other women stuck in their minds.

I glanced towards Candie. Could the mall manager have killed Theo to avoid the downfall of the mall? She nodded as if she was thinking the same thing.

CHAPTER SEVENTEEN

The next two hours flew by with talk of the holidays and if we were all prepared for Christmas. A few Loopy Ladies had last-minute shopping to do, like Susan, whose Robby and Molly had seen a toy on television that Santa *had* to bring them. She hoped the hunt for this *must-have* toy would be a short one.

As I packed up my gear, I turned to Candie and asked, "Off to work?"

She shook her head. "No, I've taken this week off. Things are usually pretty slow this time of year at city hall anyway."

"Mark? Can he get off, too?" I grimaced as the needles circling my rug hooking frame scraped my thumb.

"I wish, but no. With a new year just around the corner, he has some projects to finish up. I've done all I can organizing them. Now it's up to him for either his approval or veto." Candie straightened up from stowing her rug hooking in the basket she used for carrying her supplies.

My phone pinged with a message. I read it and smiled. "Mom and Dad said not to hurry home, as they are going to have lunch at Maxwell's Pub with the Feinsteins."

"Isn't that where Uncle Chuck and Mr. Feinstein used to play their weekly dart nights?" Candie asked as we made our way to the door.

I glanced around the room and waved goodbye to the Loopy Ladies who were left. "Have a great Christmas if I don't see you all before then."

They wished Candie and me a merry one in return as we left The Ewe.

"To answer your question, yes. Every Tuesday night was Dart Night at the pub. I think Dad and Mr. Feinstein have found a pub in Florida to carry on their love for the game." I weaved my way through the cars parked in The Ewe's lot.

I had parked my Bug next to Candie's Mustang. I clicked open the trunk and stowed my bag. As I slammed the trunk shut, I asked my cousin, "Since we are both free, do you want to stop at Sweetie Pie's for lunch? I know we were there yesterday."

"That's a grand idea, and yesterday doesn't count since we had to leave before we could enjoy our meal. I think my stomach is telling me it wants some barbeque and sweet potato fries."

"Sounds good to me, too." It was hard to decide which restaurant in Wings Falls served the best barbeque. I loved the pulled pork sandwiches at Sweetie Pie's, and David Connors served wonderful ribs at his place, The Round Up, but then again Marybeth Higgins' brother, Clint, featured mouthwatering barbeque chicken at his restaurant, The Smiling Pig. There was great competition between the three restaurants. But it was all friendly. To decide which was the winner, Hank and I, along with Mark and Candie, thought it was our duty to patronize all three restaurants as often as possible.

It only took a matter of minutes to drive to Sweetie Pie's. The café buzzed with early lunch crowd customers. As Candie and I made our way through the crowded café, I waved to the patrons I knew. I pulled on Candie's arm when I spotted one patron I wanted to question about his involvement with Theo Sayers. My cousin stopped and looked at me with a quizzical look in her violet eyes. I nodded towards a booth at the end of the room and the occupant. We walked over to the booth and slid onto its bench. The gentleman sitting across from us looked up from the copy of the *Tribune* he had spread out on the table in front of him.

"Reading about your buddy's murder, Rob?" I asked. I couldn't keep the sarcasm out of my voice.

He glared at us from under the baseball cap pulled low over his forehead. The word *Press* was embroidered in gold letters across the front. He was as skinny as the last time I'd seen him last October at the Taste of Wings Falls, where he'd been the paper's roving reporter covering the event.

"What do you ladies want? I'm here to enjoy my lunch, and I didn't invite you two to join me." Rob picked up his paper to block us out.

Candie reached over the table and pulled it down so he could see us. With a seductive grin and her best southern accent, she drawled, "Why, sugar, that isn't very inviting of you. In fact, I'd say you're being downright ungentlemanly. Right, Sam? What would our memaw say of such behavior?"

It was all I could do to keep from laughing out loud. "You're right, Candie. Memaw would be scandalized at the way Mr. Anderson here is acting."

Rob rolled his eyes and groaned. "All right, what do you ladies want?" He glanced at his watch as if he was in a hurry. Yeah, my bet was he was in a hurry to escape our questions.

"Robbie, my cousin and I heard you may be a suspect in that dear Mr. Sayers's murder. Poor soul dying like he did, all tangled up in his Christmas decorations."

Rob shot upright in his booth seat. Candie had struck a nerve, and now I wanted to know which nerve. "That's right, Rob. We've learned you were at the Sayers's residence Saturday afternoon and had words with the victim. Were you mad enough to come back later in the evening and kill him?"

"What are you two loonies talking about? Yeah, Theo and I had an argument, but I had nothing to do with his murder," Rob spit out between clenched teeth.

"So, what was your disagreement about?" I asked.

If looks could kill, Candie and I would be on our way to my own funeral parlor. "Frankly, it's none of your business. I don't have to tell you two a thing," he said.

"Rob, I'm making it my business. I want to be sure that people I love don't get blamed for something you did," I said, tapping the worn red Formica tabletop with my fingers.

Candie reached across the table and took one of Rob's hands into hers. I noticed he was a nail biter. Was he nervous about something? "Honey, you do know her sweetheart is the lead detective on the Wings Falls Police force, and she could just whisper into his ear that she suspects you of doing her neighbor in."

Rob's face turned whiter than one of Memaw's sheets, if that were possible, as he already looked as if his face had never seen a ray of sunshine. "You wouldn't?"

Was I mistaken, or was there a slight tremble in his voice?

I nodded. "Oh, yes, I would. I'll do anything to protect my loved ones," I said, thinking of my dad and Mr. Feinstein.

Rob ran a hand over his forehead, causing his hat to tilt back on his head. "All right, I went to see Theo earlier on Saturday to discuss an article he was writing—or, rather, I was writing."

Candie and I both frowned. "Who was writing the article? You or him?" I asked.

"I was, I mean…am, but he stole it from me. I went over to Theo's house to confront him about it. The last thing I heard about him was what came over my police scanner concerning a homicide at his residence."

"What do you mean, you were writing this article? What is it about?" I asked. Rob was talking double talk right now. Was he trying to confuse the matter so we wouldn't suspect him of murder?

"It will be a bombshell article about the landfill. That's all I'm going to say. Now if you ladies don't mind, I want to be left in peace." He raised his newspaper in front of his face once again, a final dismissal to Candie and me.

I swiveled in my seat towards Candie and shrugged. She answered me with one of her own. We slid out of the booth, but before we moved on to another table, I said to Rob, "I'll be sure to pass this info on to my boyfriend. I'm sure he'd like to know all about what you've told us."

His reply was a grunt from behind the newspaper.

"Okay, what do you make of what Rob told us? Do you think he killed Mr. Sayers?" Candie asked.

We were seated in our favorite booth next to the window. Dottie, our waitress, had taken our order of pulled pork sandwiches and sweet potato fries. We were sipping our coffees while waiting for the food to arrive.

I placed my mug on the table before me and flipped the fork between my fingers. "He could have. I mean, how important was this article to Rob? He said it was a bombshell. Was it big enough to win him a Pulitzer? I could see him getting angry enough and doing something drastic if he thought this article was being stolen from him."

"Wait a minute… Remember Uncle Chuck and Mr. Sayers were arguing before they escorted him out of your house. He and Mr. Feinstein both worked at the landfill years ago. They might know what this is all about."

CHAPTER EIGHTEEN

————

I swiped my lips with a paper napkin and leaned back on the cushion of my booth. "As usual, that was a great lunch. I'd better get along home. Porkchop will need to go out, and I'm hoping Mom and Dad will be home soon."

I glanced around the café. Every table was full of diners enjoying their meals. Many, I presumed, were holiday shoppers. A festive air filled the restaurant. Franny had hung red and green lights around the pass-through window into the kitchen. Shimmery bells, sleighs, and bows were taped to the walls.

Candie took a final sip of her coffee. "I need to get over to Fur Babies. I have some last-minute shopping to do for Annie and Dixie."

I rolled my eyes. Fur Babies was the town's upscale pet store and, according to Candie, the go-to place for the latest must-have fashions for a person's pet. I couldn't imagine her cat and pup needing another outfit or toy, but then again, like me, my cousin had no human children, so her pets took their place.

"What do they need now? They're already the most spoiled pets in Wings Falls." I had made a stop at the pet store earlier this month and bought Annie a pink sweater with a faux fur–trimmed hood. Dixie, while she tolerated the occasional outfit Candie slipped on her, I felt would prefer a catnip-filled toy to bat around the floor.

My Porkchop wasn't particularly impressed with the latest doggie wear. Throw a sweatshirt on him to keep out the cold when he trotted outside to do his business, and he was a happy pup. I was lucky he didn't fuss when I dressed him up for our book signing appearances.

I reached across my seat for my black Michael Kors purse and rummaged into my purse for my wallet, pulled out money for a tip, and tucked it under my coffee mug. I slid out of the booth and plucked my coat from the hook at the end. I put it on then grabbed the bill for my meal off the table. Candie did the same then followed me to the cash register to pay for our meals. I waved to Aaron, Hank's brother, who was framed in the pass-through window to the kitchen. "See you on Christmas?" I asked. Hank, Aaron, and Joy were joining my parents, Candie, and Mark for Christmas dinner at my house. Thank heavens Mom had volunteered to cook the meal, or else it would have been frozen pizza with me in charge of the menu. She, at least, had inherited Memaw Parker's cooking talent.

Aaron nodded and called back, "I'll bring dessert."

"Can you give me a hint of what it will be?" I asked. Dessert was always my favorite part of any meal.

"Nope, it's a surprise." Aaron laughed. It amazed me how much he looked like his older brother, right down to the wayward curl that fell over his forehead.

On the way to our cars, I noticed Rob Anderson sitting in his rusted and dented vehicle, having what looked like a heated conversation with someone on his phone.

I nudged Candie in the side. "Look over there. It looks like the star reporter isn't happy with someone. Do you think it could have something to do with Mr. Sayers's death and the article Rob referred to?"

"It could be, but I was thinking about what Anita Plum said this morning at Loopy Ladies."

I must have had a blank look on my face, as Candie let out an exasperated sigh. I searched my memory for that conversation. So much had been discussed by the ladies it all ran together, but then it clicked. "Oh, you mean about the mall manager possibly getting ready to fire Mr. Sayers."

Candie's auburn curls bounced about her shoulders as she nodded. "Yes. Anita said that Mr. Sayers was acting inappropriately towards some of the kids' mothers and one dad was threatening to sue. What if the mall manager's job was on the line because of a certain nasty Santa?"

"Yes. I can see where the manager would be mad enough at Mr. Sayers if he thought he could lose his job because of his un-Santa-like behavior. Who knows what the manager's life is like? Maybe he really needs his job, especially now during the holidays when there are so many more expenses. Are you doing anything after work tomorrow?"

Candie shook her head. "Remember? I'm off this week."

"Oh, that's right. Sorry, I'm just a little rattled. I don't like the fact that Dad was questioned twice by the police. They must feel he's a possible suspect, even though he is taking it pretty lightly. With Joe Peters involved, I don't trust him. You know he'd love to lock me up and throw away the key. My dad would be the next best thing to pinning a murder on me."

My phone pinged. I slipped my hand into my coat pocket to retrieve my phone and read the text. *Sam, help!! Please, I need your help. Can I meet you at your house ASAP? Love, Hank*

My hands shook, and I could feel the blood drain out of my face. What happened to my unflappable Hank to send this message? I tapped in his number, but it went to his voice mail.

Candie slid an arm around my shoulder. "Sweetie, what happened? You look like you've seen a ghost, and you're shaking like a leaf."

I turned my phone so she could read Hank's message. Candie's eyes widened. "Now, sugar, don't go jumping to conclusions. His message could mean anything. Maybe he needs help picking out a Christmas present for his mother."

A smile curved my lips. Leave it to my cousin to shine a bright light on a situation, no matter how dire, as I feared this one was. "Oh, Candie, if only life was as bright as you see it."

"What's the use of looking on the dark side of things? It won't solve any problems, not like a little sunshine will."

I hugged my cousin then reached for the door handle of my Bug. "I'd better get home and see what this is all about," I said, motioning the phone towards her.

Candie leaned over and kissed my cheek. "All will be well, sugar, I know it will. I won't let it be any other way."

I got into my car, rolled down the window, then waved to her as I backed out of my parking place. "I love you. I'll call later and tell you what this is all about."

"You'd better," she said, opening her car door and slipping behind the wheel.

I beeped the horn as I drove out of Sweetie Pie's parking lot.

Ten minutes later, I pulled into my driveway and parked behind Gladys's car and Hank's Jeep. As I walked up the brick path to my house, I heard Porkchop barking and what sounded like squeals and laughter from young children coming from inside my house. Who could be visiting? Other than my fellow Loopy Lady, Susan Mayfield, who had two small children, I didn't have any friends with young children. Since I didn't see her car in my drive, who could be visiting?

I slid the strap of my purse farther up my shoulder and turned the knob to my front door. I was stunned at what greeted me when I stepped into my entryway.

CHAPTER NINETEEN

———

Mom and Dad relaxed on my sofa with happy grins on their faces. Hank sat cross-legged on the floor with Porkchop barking and two preschoolers climbing on his shoulders and lap.

"Hank?" I asked, a puzzled look on my face.

He looked up at me, his wavy hair mussed and a smile on his face. He was obviously enjoying the roughhousing as much as the giggling children.

Before he could answer, Mom said, "Aren't they precious? What fun it will be to have them for a few days. Christmas means so much more when you enjoy it with children. Don't you agree, Chuck?"

Dad wore a sweater. A palm tree design with plastic Christmas balls hanging from its branches was on the front. "You're right, Babs. I remember how much we loved the holidays when Sam was little like these two." He nodded towards the two boys climbing on Hank's shoulders. "And still believed in Santa Claus."

Hank placed the children on the floor and stood up. He ran a hand through his mussed hair. "Eli, Landon, I need to talk to Sam for a few minutes." He picked up one of Porkchop's squeaky toys off the floor and handed it to the boys. "Maybe you two can toss this for Porkchop to fetch."

Eli and Landon were just two of the many nephews of Hank's I'd met and grown to love since dating him.

"Hank, you take your time to explain your dilemma to Sam. Chuck and I can watch your nephews while you two talk. Since we don't have grandchildren, this will be a real treat for us." Mom tugged on her sweater. It matched my dad's. She'd paired hers with pink skinny pants. They certainly were a change from what I called her "mom jeans" she used to wear.

Hank led me into my den and shut the door behind him. My anxiety rose as I took in the serious look on his face. I sank onto the loveseat. He sat next to me. His hands dangled between his knees as he stared at the blue braided rug on the floor.

I reached over and took one of his strong hands into mine. "Hank, what is this all about, and why aren't you at work instead of playing with your nephews on my living room floor?"

"That's just it, Sam. I *was* at work, but then I got an urgent call from my mom."

My heart thudded in my chest. What could have happened? Was someone ill or had they had an accident? *Please Lord, don't have anything have happened to his family,* I silently prayed. "What did she say?"

He straightened in his seat and looked at me. Worry clouded his eyes. "Mom is in Illinois taking care of her sister, Diana, who had a hip replacement."

I nodded. This wasn't anything new to me. Hank had told me his mom would be out of town taking care of his aunt. "Yes, you told me that a few weeks ago. So where is your sister?" Amelia was the boys' mother and my favorite of Hank's six siblings.

"That's just it. You know she's pregnant and due in a few weeks."

"Yes, we're all looking forward to this New Year's baby." Even though I'd never had children, a new baby was a blessing, and I anticipated this newest addition to Hank's family as much as he did.

"Amelia is having a few complications, and her doctor has placed her on bed rest. I've told you about her husband, Matt, who is in the Army and stationed overseas. He was coming home in January for the baby's birth, but with this development, the Army is giving him leave to fly home early. Mom called my aunt Diana's daughter, and she's going to fly to Illinois and take over for Mom so she can watch the boys until Amelia's husband arrives here."

My heart went out to Amelia. To go through this without her husband must be devastating. "What can I do? Who's helping her now?"

The look on his face tore at my heart. "She has a good friend who has volunteered to check in on her until Mom can get here, but she can't take care of the boys. Sam, could the boys stay with you until Mom arrives home? It should only be for a day or two. I hate to do this to you, but everyone else in the family is either tied up with their own family or is out of town for the holidays."

I gulped. Me? Watch two young boys? I had zero, zippo experience dealing with kids other than reading to them when Porkchop and I did a book signing, and then they had their parents to tend to them if they got a bit antsy. "Ummm, Hank, are you sure you want me to watch them?"

He pulled me into his arms. "I couldn't think of anyone I'd trust them with more than you. I wish this murder investigation wasn't taking up so much of my time and I didn't have to thrust this on you."

Tears leaked out of my eyes. His comment touched me deeply, as he had been married before and his pregnant wife was murdered. She had been an investigative reporter and was covering one last story before she went on maternity leave. She was doing a story on gang activity and died from a stray bullet when she got caught in the crossfire of rival gangs. Hank was ten years younger than my fifty-six years. Occasionally, the thought worried me that he'd regret being involved with me since I was well past my baby-making years and would never be able to give him a child.

Laughter and squeals floated through the closed den door.

"I certainly will have a lot of help entertaining them," I said, thinking of how much Mom and Dad would enjoy having the boys with us.

"Thank you," Hank said, leaning over and kissing me.

"We'd better go rescue my parents," I said, pushing off the loveseat.

Hank hesitated a moment before standing up. I turned to him and, with a raised eyebrow, asked, "What's the matter, Hank? Is something else bothering you?"

A chill ran through me. I could feel it in my bones that something serious was on his mind and I wouldn't like his answer.

"You know we took Mr. Sayers's laptop down to the station to see if there was anything on it that would help us find his murderer," he said, running a hand through his hair. A wayward brown curl fell over his forehead. I reached up and brushed it back.

"Yes, I do. Did you find anything important?" Hank's behavior was making me more nervous by the second.

He raised his crystal blue eyes to mine. "Mr. Sayers was writing an article about the landfill where your dad and Mr. Feinstein worked."

I frowned, remembering Mr. Sayers mentioning that when he was here during the Christmas party.

"It appears the owner of the landfill was allowing a local construction company, Ferguson Construction, to dump hazardous materials there, and they have now leached into the ground and contaminated it."

My eyes widened in surprise. "That's the company who built my house. How long has this been going on?"

"It's hard to tell, but we think a long time… Probably years," Hank said, holding my hands in his.

"So do you think the owner of the landfill may have gotten wind of this article and murdered Mr. Sayers to prevent him from publishing it?" I asked, shocked by what Hank was telling me.

Hank shrugged. "We're not sure. We questioned the landfill owner, and he says he had no knowledge of this happening and blames two of his workers. He says they probably were being paid off by the construction company to allow the dumping. Then again, Mr. Connors has been in poor health and has left the running of the landfill to his wife and daughter."

I started to tremble after hearing what Hank said. "Let me guess… He accused my dad and Mr. Feinstein of being the employees who took the bribes from this Ferguson Construction Company to allow for this illegal waste dumping?"

"I'm afraid so, Sam."

CHAPTER TWENTY

―――――

I collapsed back onto the loveseat. "What?" I screeched. "Where does that man get off accusing my dad and his friend of being crooks? Especially after all these years of being a dedicated employee. Dad rarely called in sick and would cover for other guys who did." I felt my blood pressure rising. It'd be a miracle if Hank didn't have to rush me to the hospital for a stroke. Wouldn't I love spending my Christmas unwrapping presents in a hospital bed?

A thought struck me. "Wait a minute. Candie and I visited Mrs. Sayers, and she said Rob Anderson stopped by her house earlier in the day and he and her husband had a huge argument."

Hank sat up straighter on the loveseat. "Argument? She never mentioned this to Officer Greensleeves when she questioned Mrs. Sayers. I'll have to send an officer over to ask her about this disagreement between the two men. Oh, and why did you and Candie go over to Mrs. Sayers's house? You're not poking your pretty little nose into this investigation, are you?" Hank tapped the end of my nose with his finger.

I cringed, knowing he'd said the same thing to me on more than one occasion, even once already since Mr. Sayers's murder. Since my father and Mr. Feinstein were now involved, I knew I'd be doing the same for them.

When I didn't reply right away, he asked, "Sam, what have you been up to?"

I stared down at my hands. My fingers fumbled with the edge of my sweater. "Nothing, really."

Hank tilted my head up so he could look me directly in the eyes. "Sam, I know you. You're as loyal to your friends and family as Porkchop is to you. When one of them is in trouble, you want to make everything right for them. I love this quality in you, but it scares me to death at the same time."

"Okay, Candie and I were doing the neighborly thing and brought Mrs. Sayers a plate of brownies. She happened to mention that Rob Anderson stopped by their house on Saturday and he and Mr. Sayers argued. We also stopped by Sweetie Pie's for a bite to eat today and happened to run into Rob Anderson, so we sat down and chatted with him." There, I'd said it. I didn't want to implicate Rosa Sayers. I had a stronger feeling Rob was the murderer.

A smile curved Hank's lips "A chat or a grilling?"

I laughed. He knew me so well. "I'll call it a chat, but he said that Mr. Sayers stole this article from him. Candie and I think Rob feels this article would put him in the running for winning the Pulitzer Prize." *In his dreams was more like it,* I thought.

Hank tapped the side of his head, contemplating what I had told him. "Interesting. So, if he felt he would lose out on the big prize because of Mr. Sayers ripping off his article, he might take drastic action to prevent this from happening. I think a visit to Mr. Anderson is in order."

I patted Hank's knee. "You and I both know my dad and his friend are innocent. Come on. Let's get back to the living room and see what the boys and my parents are up to. From the sounds of all the laughter, they must be having a good time."

Hank stood then held out a hand to help me stand. Before he released it, he pulled me into his arms. "I know that with all of your company, we don't have much alone time. Just know I love you with all my heart." He tapped the gold heart-shaped necklace I'd worn every day since he gave it to me at Candie and Mark's wedding last summer. "Never forget the inscription on the back. *MTYLTT.*"

I nodded. "More Than Yesterday Less Than Tomorrow."

"Yes. I love you More Than Yesterday But Less Than Tomorrow. Never forget that, Sam." He bent his head and gave me a kiss that let me know he meant what he said.

As we walked back into the living room, my heart swelled with love for my parents. I couldn't help but laugh.

"Dad, are you sure you should be doing that? I mean, your back and all?" I said, watching him crawl around the room with a giggling Landon on his back, treating the small boy to a horsey ride. I sucked in my breath as they pranced a little too close to the Christmas tree. The ornaments Hank and I had so carefully hung on the tree swayed back and forth.

"Hi, Muffin. The boys are having a great time with your mom and me. Right, Landon?"

"Uh-huh," agreed Landon, nodding with a huge grin on his face as he sat on Dad's back. I feared how Dad would feel come morning after serving as a horse. It was a good many years since he'd acted as my personal horsey, and his bones were a lot younger then.

"Me, too," piped up Eli, who sat on the sofa next to my mom. She was reading my book *Porkchop, the Wonder Dog* to him. The star of the book lay curled up next to Eli as the boy idly stroked my pup's back.

I smiled. The happy look on Eli's face as my mom read to him was the reason I loved to write for children.

"Boys, I'm real busy at work, so until Nana comes home from your aunt Diana's, you're going to spend a couple of days with Sam and her parents. I know you'll love visiting them." Hank looked at me for backup.

"Yes, and you can call your mom whenever you want," I said, knowing the boys would miss their mother something fierce.

Landon slid off Dad's back, and Eli hopped off the sofa. "Yippee," they shouted. They joined hands and jumped around in a circle. I held my breath as the ornaments on the tree bounced up and down. Rudolph slid precariously towards the end of his branch. "Aunt Barbara and Uncle Chuck are so much fun."

"Aunt Barbara and Uncle Chuck?" I whispered, reaching in and rehanging the reindeer.

Hank shrugged. "If they don't mind, I don't. Do you?"

I shook my head. This was as close as they were going to get to having young children around to enjoy, and it was the time of year meant for kids. Plus, the boys would keep my parents occupied while I proved my dad innocent of murdering Mr. Sayers.

Mom glanced over at me. "The boys are going to stay with us for a couple of days?"

I nodded and explained to her what Hank had relayed to me in the den about their mom's situation. Of course, in front of the little guys, I downplayed the seriousness of the matter.

Mom nodded. She understood what I was saying. The boys, on the other hand, only heard that their dad would be home for Christmas. They jumped up and down with excitement again.

"Santa heard me," Eli screamed.

"Santa heard you?" I asked, puzzled at what he was referring to.

"Yes, before Nana went to see Aunt Diana, she helped me write my letter to Santa, and I asked him to bring my daddy home for Christmas," he said, his face beaming with excitement.

If this wasn't a Hallmark moment, I didn't know what was. Smiles spread across the boys' faces, and their bodies shook with joy at the thought their dad would be home for Christmas.

"Guys, you have to be really good for Sam and her mom and dad. Okay? Santa is still watching you," Hank cautioned his nephews.

Their blond curls bounced as they nodded. "We will. We promise. Can we call Mommy and talk to her?" Even though they'd been preoccupied with my parents, their mom was still on their minds.

I knelt in front of the two. While they may be only a year apart, the only thing they shared was their hair coloring and curls. Eli was at least two inches taller than Landon. Landon had the same crystal blue eyes as his uncle Hank, but Eli's were a rich chocolate brown. "Remember, I told you fellows you can call Mommy anytime you like, and I meant it."

A thought struck me. I could kill two birds with one stone. "Have you been to the mall yet to visit Santa Claus?"

They shook their heads. "Mommy hasn't been feeling too good lately, so she hasn't been able to take us."

"How would you like to go tomorrow and give Santa the letters you wrote?"

Both boys whooped with delight and threw their arms around me. I glanced up to see Hank looking at me with a raised eyebrow. He knew me too well and figured there was more to my seemingly innocent invitation to visit the jolly old man.

CHAPTER TWENTY-ONE

After a fun evening with Hank's nephews, they settled in bed in my spare bedroom with their favorite toys. Eli had his arms wrapped around a plush teddy, and Landon snuggled with Woody from the *Toy Story* movie. I glanced down at the boys' sweet faces and wished their world could remain forever innocent as it was now.

"What are you thinking?" Hank asked as he slid his arm around my shoulders and pulled me against his side.

I let out a deep sigh. "How peaceful they look sleeping and wishing they could always keep their youthful innocence."

Hank bent and kissed the top of my head. "I'll do my best to help them hold on to their dreams as long as possible."

I turned into his arms. "You're a great uncle, you know?"

"Aww, thanks, ma'am," Hank said. A blush colored his face.

I playfully punched his arm. "Speaking of kids, let's see what my parents are up to."

He laughed. "After we check on them, I'd better get back to the station and see what I can do about solving Theo's murder."

We headed in the direction of the den, where we found my parents snuggled up on the loveseat watching *It's a Wonderful Life*, a favorite Christmas movie we'd watched every year when I was younger.

Hank stuck his head in the door. "Night, Chuck and Barbara."

Startled, they drew apart. "Night, Hank. Will we see you tomorrow?"

Hank nodded. "I hope so, but I can't promise anything. Thanks for watching the boys until my mom gets home."

"Oh, we'll have so much fun, won't we, Chuck?" Mom looked into my dad's face for confirmation.

Dad caressed Mom's cheek. "Yes, we will. After all, kids put the fun in Christmas."

My heart did a flip. Did they regret I'd never given them grandchildren? I hoped not.

Hank held my hand as we walked to my front door. When we arrived there, I dug in the closet for his down vest.

As he slipped it on, he said, "Wait here while I run out to my car and get the boys' booster seats."

"Booster seats?" I asked. I wasn't familiar with all the equipment kids needed.

"Yeah, in New York once they outgrow their car seats, they need a booster seat to ride in."

"Oh." I shivered from the blast of cold air that entered the house when he opened the door and stepped outside. Kids certainly didn't travel light. Luckily, Hank had come prepared tonight with the boys' small suitcases and favorite toys. He knew I would never have said no to his request to watch them.

Minutes later, he stepped back into the house holding the two seats. "You place them on the back seat of the car and buckle the guys in."

I could handle this. They seemed simple enough. "We'll take Gladys's car to the mall when we go out tomorrow to visit Santa. It's bigger than my Bug." I inwardly groaned at the thought of driving Gladys's "love machine." Maybe I could wear a scarf around the lower part of my face and no one would recognize me.

Hank laughed. "Oh, yes, your visit to Santa. You won't be doing a bit of sleuthing while you're there, would you?"

I feigned an innocent look. "Would I do that?"

A grin spread across his face. "The Nancy Drew of Wings Falls? Why would such an idea even enter my mind? Please, be careful." With that, he pulled me into his arms and gave me a kiss. "I love you, Sam," he said then opened the door and walked down my front steps to his car. He had jockeyed cars around earlier so mine now resided in the garage and his sat behind Gladys's.

* * *

"Are you guys ready to visit Santa?" I asked, from the driver's seat of Gladys's car. My dad had opted out of our trip to the mall. He said he'd made plans to hang out with Herb Feinstein today. They'd contacted some of their buddies from when they'd worked at the landfill and were going to spend the afternoon hanging out with them.

"Yes" was the resounding answer from the back seat. I glanced over my shoulder at the boys squirming with excitement. They looked as if they would burst if we didn't get to the mall soon.

"Are you boys warm enough?" Mom asked from the passenger seat. She'd made sure they had donned their scarves, hats, and mittens before they left the house. I had a feeling they'd be shedding them once the warmth of the mall hit them.

"Yes, Aunt Barbara," they said in unison.

I turned the car on, placed it in gear, and backed out of the driveway. The mall was only a short drive from my house.

"Is Candie going to meet us at the mall?" Mom asked.

"Yes. I called her this morning, and she said she'd be there. She has some last-minute shopping to do for Mark," I said, stopping at a red light. There were a few things I needed to pick up for Hank, too, like the baby blue turtleneck sweater I'd spied in the window of the mall's men's store. It was a perfect match to his eyes. "How about you, Mom? Anything else you need to buy?" The light changed, and we continued on while the boys chatted in the back seat about what they wanted Santa to bring.

"No, I'm fine. I've got everything, but I need to wrap the presents," Mom said.

"I've got plenty of wrapping paper, so don't bother to buy any."

"Oh, thanks, sweetie. That was the one thing I hoped you had. I certainly didn't want to cart any on the plane."

I flipped on my turn signal. We'd arrived at the entrance to the mall. "It looks like everyone in Wings Falls and all the surrounding towns had the same idea as we did today." I nodded towards the parking lot.

Mom's mouth formed on *O.* "It certainly is crowded."

A plea came from the back seat. "We can still see Santa, can't we?"

"Absolutely, no matter what. Then afterwards maybe we can have lunch at one of the mall's restaurants," Mom said, twisting towards the back seat.

Another youthful cheer went up from the boys.

I was lucky to score a parking space not far from the mall's entrance. As I put the car into park, my phone buzzed with a text message. I glanced at it to see it was from Candie.

Meet me by Santa.

Mom raised a quizzical eyebrow.

"It's from Candie. She's already here and waiting for us by Santa," I said, placing my phone in the front pocket of my red Vera Bradley purse.

Mom and I climbed out of the car and opened the rear doors to unbuckle the boys' seat belts. "Hold our hands. We don't want to lose you among all the people today," I instructed the boys. That would be all I needed, to have to call Hank and tell him we couldn't find his nephews.

Eli and Landon laughed.

"What's so funny, boys?" I asked as we walked through the crowded parking lot towards the entrance.

"You sound like our mom," Eli said. He skipped beside me, his small hand clutched in mine.

"Wow. You'd think it was a Black Friday sale going on," Mom said as we navigated our way through the crowded mall on our way to see Santa. Shoppers bumped into us loaded down with shopping bags bursting with their purchases.

"It's not too crowded for us to see Santa, is it?" Landon asked. A frown furrowed his forehead.

"Excuse me," I said as I bumped into a shopper. I had Eli's hand in a death grip for fear he'd be yanked away from me and I'd never find him in this sea of people. "Nope. I have it on good authority Santa is waiting for the two of you."

"Really?" Landon asked, his eyes wide with amazement.

"Really," I replied. I crossed my fingers and prayed Santa wasn't on a coffee break when we got to him.

"Over here. Sam, over here," I heard my cousin's voice calling to me.

I turned in the direction of the shouter and laughed. "There's Candie, and she's sitting on Santa's lap."

With her arms wrapped around Santa's neck, she smiled at the elf snapping her picture. Oh good. The elf was one of the people I wanted to talk to while we visited with Santa.

CHAPTER TWENTY-TWO

―――――

"Who are these precious young men?" Candie rose from Santa's lap, bent down, and shook Eli and Landon's hands.

"They're Hank's nephews," I said, giving her an abbreviated version why the boys were with Mom and me. I'd been so busy with the boys, I hadn't had time to call her about Hank's text. For the boys' benefit, I, again, left out the serious version of why their mother couldn't watch them right now.

I introduced Eli and Landon to Candie.

"Well, sugars, Santa told me he has been waiting all morning to see you two young'uns."

Their eyes widened and filled with a look of awe. "Really, he's been waiting just for us?"

Her earrings, Christmas wreaths that flashed on and off, swung back and forth as she nodded. "Really. Hop in line so you can talk to him." She pointed to the growing line of young children who waited to see Santa.

The boys did as they were instructed and joined the other children. Eli's and Landon's bodies shook with excitement. I turned to my mom. "Mom, can you stand with the boys for a few minutes? I want to talk to Anita Plum's daughters."

"Sure, sweetheart. Where are they?" she replied, looking around the Santa-designated area.

I pointed to two elves. One elf handled the money if the parents wanted their child's picture taken, and elf number two snapped their pictures.

Candie followed me over to the festive table they stood next to.

"Hi, Susie and Sara," I said.

They had a blank look in their eyes.

"Oh, you don't remember me. I'm Sam Reynolds. I rug hook with your mom. And this is my cousin, Candie," I said, flicking my thumb in her direction. "She also hooks with your mom."

Recognition dawned on the girls. I'd only met them a few times when the Loopy Ladies held a summer barbeque or party where the whole family was invited. I hadn't seen the girls in a few years. I guess hanging out with a bunch of hookers wasn't a cool thing for teens to do. They had certainly grown since the last time I'd seen them. Even dressed in their elf costumes of tights and oversized sweaters, they'd matured into lovely young women. Sara's blonde hair flowed down her back, while Susie had her red hair styled in a short pixie cut that framed her delicate features.

"Oh, hi, Sam. Now I know who you are. You have that cute doggie. What's his name? Porkchop?" Sara asked.

I nodded. "That's him." People may not remember me, but Porkchop was unforgettable.

I glanced over at the line of children waiting for Santa to make sure Eli and Landon were behaving for my mom. They were busy chatting with each other. Excitement was written all over their faces.

"What can we do for you, Sam?" Sara asked.

I stepped aside so she could take money from a parent who wanted their child's picture snapped with Santa. Susie was busy waving a stuffed teddy bear in the air so the child sitting on Santa's lap would look at her camera.

"I'm watching my boyfriend's nephews for a day or two, so I brought them to the mall to see Santa. I'd like to have their pictures taken with the jolly one."

Sara laughed then pointed to the various picture packages displayed on the table in front of her available to purchase. I gulped when she mentioned the prices. Santa was no longer a freebie Polaroid snapshot given to the parents after their child finished telling Santa what they wanted under the tree.

I pointed to the least expensive photo option and pulled my credit card out of my wallet and handed it to her. I leaned over to Candie and whispered to her, "I'm going to try and get some info out of Sara."

She nodded and said, "Go for it. I'll help your mom with the boys."

"So, Sara. Is that a different Santa from when I was here at the mall last week?" Might as well get right to the reason I was here.

Sara had rung up my purchase and handed me back my card. "Yeah, and thank heavens."

Teens certainly didn't beat around the bush. "Why do you say that? Wasn't he very good with the children?"

"He was fine with the kids, but it was the moms and Susie and me he bothered."

Sara turned to another parent who wanted her attention to pay for their child's picture package.

After Sara completed the transaction, she leaned over the table and in a hushed voice said, "He was a dirty old man."

Okay, now I was getting somewhere. I asked, "How so?"

"He thought he was acting funny telling Susie and me his nasty, dirty jokes. He wasn't funny, only disgusting." Sara frowned. I imagined just the thought of his off-color jokes creeped her out.

"Wow, I'm sorry you had to put up with him." I feigned ignorance and asked, "Did you tell your parents?"

The bell on her elf hat jingled as she nodded. "Yeah, my dad was really steamed when we told him. I thought he'd burst a blood vessel."

"Did he do anything?" I asked. Since she was so forthcoming with her information, I thought I'd get to the heart of the matter.

"He wanted us to quit, but we told him we liked our jobs too much to let creepy Mr. Sayers make us quit. Susie wants to be a photojournalist, and I want to be a schoolteacher."

I smiled. "Just like your mom."

"Yeah, but I want to teach the younger kids. I don't know how Mom puts up with the kids at my high school." Sara's shoulders shuddered.

"So, what did your dad do? Anything?"

Sara answered a question a parent had about the photos then turned back to me. "He came to the mall last week and talked to the manager. No, make that he shouted at the manager. I think the whole mall heard what my dad had to say about Mr. Sayers."

"Did the manager talk to Mr. Sayers?" I asked. I couldn't believe how lucky I was getting this information from Sara, but then, she didn't know I was trying to dig up information to prove my dad and Mr. Feinstein innocent of Mr. Sayers's murder.

"Yeah, sort of."

"What do you mean sort of?" I asked, stepping aside to let a parent get closer to the table.

"It was more like an argument."

My ears perked up. I was really getting somewhere. "Did you hear what was said?"

"Oh yeah, and so did half the mall. The manager was really steamed. He told Mr. Sayers to leave Susie and me alone, but that wasn't all. He mentioned he'd fire Mr. Sayers if he bothered another mother, because there was a guy threatening to sue the mall. He said he wasn't about to lose his job because Santa couldn't keep his hands to himself."

"What did Mr. Sayers do for that to happen?"

"I guess he got fresh with one of the moms."

"Gross" was all I could say.

"Yeah, mega gross," Sara said.

At that moment, my mom strode up to me holding Eli's and Landon's hands.

"Sam, Sam," Eli shouted, bouncing from one foot to the other with excitement. "We got to tell Santa everything we want for Christmas."

Mom smiled down at the boys. "Yes, they were angels while waiting to see Santa. I bet they'll have lots of presents under their tree from him."

I leaned down and pushed back a lock of hair that had fallen over Eli's eyes.

"Look, Sam. See what Mrs. Claus gave us." He held up a small coloring book and box of crayons.

A smiling woman, wearing a long red dress with a lace-trimmed mop cap on her white curls and half glasses perched on her nose, stood next to Santa. She helped situate the young children on Santa's lap and handed out the gifts to the children when they finished telling Santa what they wanted him to bring for Christmas.

"That's wonderful. Mom, could you treat the guys to something to eat while Candie and I go ask a man some questions?"

Mom beamed. I think she was having as much fun as Eli and Landon. "Sure, but let me visit the little girls' room first. I'll meet you in front of the Happy Moose." She scurried off to see to her needs.

Candie raised an eyebrow. "Questions? Who are we going to quiz?"

I leaned towards her and said in a low voice that only she could hear, "Maybe the man who killed my neighbor."

Her eyebrows rose and her violet eyes widened.

CHAPTER TWENTY-THREE

"Okay boys, when my mom gets back, you are going to have lunch at the Happy Moose," I said, mentioning the mall's popular fast-food restaurant.

"Yippee," the boys, jumping up and down, shouted in unison.

"Can I have a hamburger and fries?" Eli asked, a smile spreading across his small face.

"I'd like a chocolate milk shake, puh-leease," Landon said, staring up at me with pleading eyes.

Candie leaned over to me and said, "Look at those adorable faces. How can you resist them?"

I shrugged and laughed. "That's just it. I can't." I turned to the boys. "Come on. Let's find Aunt Barbara, and she'll get you whatever you want for lunch."

Thrilled, the boys skipped alongside us as we snaked our way through the crowd of people in the mall. As we drew closer to the entrance to the Happy Moose, I saw my mom waving at us.

"Sam, Sam," she called out to me.

The boys raced the last few yards towards her. Mom knelt and scooped them into a hug.

"Aunt Barbara, I love what Mrs. Claus gave us." Eli waved the coloring book and crayons at my mom.

Mom smiled and ruffled Eli's hair. "That's wonderful. Maybe when we get home, you and Uncle Chuck can color and have some hot chocolate. You told Santa everything you wanted for Christmas, right?"

Landon nodded enthusiastically. "Yep, I told him I wanted Legos and Hot Wheels and a Bluey plushy…"

Candie turned to me and whispered, "Bluey? Who's that?"

I shrugged. "I guess a new kids' favorite toy. I was into Strawberry Shortcake and My Little Pony."

Candie laughed. "Memaw stood in line for hours to get me a Pound Puppy."

I joined in her laughter. "Yeah, she spoiled you rotten."

Candie poked me in the ribs. "Right. She didn't put up with any nonsense, and you know it."

I had to agree with my cousin. I spent the summers playing with Candie on Memaw Parker's farm and knew that even though Memaw was strict, she was also very loving.

I turned my attention back to the boys and Mom. They had finished reciting their Christmas list to her.

I hoped Mom could handle all their youthful energy while Candie and I were talking with the mall manager.

My mom laughed. "You guys ready for lunch at the Happy Moose?"

Both Eli and Landon jumped with joy and shouted, "Yes!"

Mom looked up at me. "Guess that settles it. Text me when you're ready to leave."

I hugged my mom and said I would.

As Candie and I walked away, she asked. "So where are we going?"

"To the mall manager's office," I said, dodging a shopper who was too busy talking on her cell phone to look where she was going.

"Do I want to know why we are going there?" Candie asked as we wove our way through the crowd of shoppers.

I relayed to her my suspicions about the mall manager and why I thought he might have a reason to kill Mr. Sayers.

"So, good ole Theo was a dirty old Santa? Shame on him for tarnishing Santa's image. I don't blame Anita's husband for being riled up at Theo telling his daughters nasty jokes. Santa certainly would have put him on his naughty list if Mr. Sayers hit on a mother, too. Mr. Sayers didn't know when to stop, did he?"

"We need a reason to speak to the mall manager. We can't start out with 'So, did you kill Santa?'"

Candie placed a hand on my arm. I stopped and turned to her. "Sugar, leave it to me. I'll come up with something."

I smiled. My cousin would have the man eating out of her hand before he knew what hit him.

The offices were tucked in a hallway near a side entrance to the mall. A set of bells hung from the door handle and jingled when I pushed open the glass door. A young woman wearing a Santa hat nestled amongst her curly hair sat behind a desk. A name plate stating she was Ms. Allen rested on the desk amidst a pile of papers. She was busy talking on the phone as we approached her desk. She looked up at us, smiled, and held up one finger, indicating she'd be with us in a minute. Candie and I nodded and took two of the metal seats along the wall opposite her desk. We waited patiently for her to end her conversation.

Ms. Allen hung up the phone and tucked a stray curl back under her hat. "Sorry. What can I do for you two? This place has been crazy since that Santa was killed. There's one reporter who keeps bugging us. He wants to know what we know about Santa. I mean, the Santa only worked part-time. It's not like he hung out in the office here. But that's not your problem."

I looked at Candie and mouthed, *Rob?*

Candie nodded. She stood and approached the desk. "Honey, those reporters can be real pesky, can't they? But, sugar, my cousin and I would love to talk to your manager about doing a book signing."

Ms. Allen leaned towards us. She looked around as if to see if anyone was listening to her. Ignoring Candie's request to do a book signing, she said, "Tell me about the press. It's not like I don't have enough to handle with how busy the mall is during the holiday season, especially since that Santa was causing us a number of headaches. If it wasn't for the fact there's a Santa shortage, Howie would have fired him long ago."

Discretion was not Ms. Allen's middle name. She was eager to spread all the mall gossip.

I rose from my chair and joined Candie in front of the desk. "Howie?" I asked.

Ms. Allen fidgeted with a pen on the desk. "He's the mall manager. He was dealing with a number of complaints about the deceased Santa."

Candie looked at her, wide-eyed. "Complaints about Santa? Isn't he supposed to be a jolly old man? Who would have issues with him?"

"Yeah, you would think, wouldn't you?" Ms. Allen stopped in mid thought and straightened in her seat. "Oh, hi, Howie. These ladies would like to see you if you have a moment."

I turned to see a forty-something man walk in the office and approach the desk. The sleeves of his maroon striped dress shirt were rolled up to his elbows. His tie, decorated with a Christmas tree, hung loose about his neck. He ran a hand through his dirty-blond hair and gave us a harried look.

"What can I do for you ladies? I hope there aren't any problems." He turned to Ms. Allen. "I thought we were through with any issues once Theo was gone."

She shrugged and studied her nails with great interest.

I looked at Candie and raised my eyebrows. How desperate was this Howie to make sure the mall ran smoothly? Desperate enough to get rid of the reason for the mall's troubles?

CHAPTER TWENTY-FOUR

———

Candie gave Howie a wide smile and batted her long eyelashes at him. She held out her slim hand for him to shake and turned on the full force of her Southern charm. "Why, sugar, my cousin, here, Samantha Davies, and I want to give you the grand opportunity to host two very successful authors at this here fine mall of yours."

My eyes widened at my cousin's statement. Successful? At least not yet for me, but hopefully, on my way. Still, Howie was under Candie's spell. I wanted to snap my fingers in front of his eyes and lift his jaw off the floor. I was surprised drool didn't drip from the sides of his mouth. Instead, I coughed, which seemed to bring him back to his surroundings.

"Ummm, sure. Ladies, why don't we talk about this in my office. Ms. Allen, please hold my calls."

The receptionist looked up from inspecting her nails and nodded. "Sure, Howie, but don't forget you have a phone conference in thirty minutes with the owner of the mall."

Howie groaned. "Yeah, at least I can tell him the source of all our problems is gone and there shouldn't be any further trouble. At least not from Santa."

He escorted us into his office. It was a very sparsely furnished room, dominated by a metal desk in the center and three chairs—a cushioned swivel one behind the desk and two molded plastic chairs in front of it. The walls were bare of any decoration. A tan metal file cabinet hugged the far wall. Folders littered the top of the desk. And a wire trash can rested on the tile floor. The only thing to personalize this space were the pictures of a woman holding the hands of two small boys placed on the edge of the desk.

He snagged a down coat off the back of one plastic chair before walking around the desk and draping it over the swivel chair. "Ladies, please have a seat and tell me about the books you have written. I'm afraid I don't have much time to read with my busy schedule, so I may not be familiar with your work."

Candie scooted forward on her seat towards Howie's desk. "Sugar, I write an extremely popular romance series. In fact, my latest book, *Hot Night in Paradise,* is an Amazon bestseller. My cousin, here, Samantha Davies, is the author of the hit children's book, *Porkchop, the Wonder Dog.*

Howie leaned his arms on his desk and nodded thoughtfully. "Can't say I've heard of them, but that doesn't mean anything. As I said, with my job as this mall's manager and my family, it leaves little time for reading."

I pointed toward the picture on his desk. "Is that your family?"

He smiled. "Yeah, my wife and two sons, Desmond and Barry. They were a bit younger in that picture. They're in Wings Falls Junior High now and very involved in sports. You know, baseball, football, swimming. You name it, they love it."

"Phew-wee. Darlin, you must be kept very busy," Candie said, waving her ruby-painted fingernails in front of her face.

Howie nodded. "You don't know the half of it. They're also on traveling teams for each sport."

"I don't have any kids, but I guess it must get expensive," I said, wondering how desperate Howie might be to maintain the peace in the mall. An overfriendly Santa might jeopardize his job, and there would go the money needed to keep his boys involved in the sports they loved.

Howie pushed aside a pile of folders and flipped open a calendar. He picked up a pen and poised it over the calendar. "Yes, it does, but back to you ladies and your books. When would you be available for book signings? It would probably have to be after Christmas because it is only a few days away."

"Since my books ooze romance, how about February? You know, Valentine's Day? What works for you, Sam?" Candie asked, turning towards me.

"Well, I can't say *Porkchop, the Wonder Dog* 'oozes romance,' but it would be a fun addition to a child's Easter basket. When is Easter next year?" I asked, leaning towards Howie's desk.

He flipped over a page in his calendar and glanced up at me. "It's early next year, in March. How about the beginning of the month?"

"Sounds good to me," I said then added, "Oh, by the way, was the mall busy last Saturday night?"

Howie frowned. "Yeah, from what I heard it was crazy with last-minute shoppers."

"You weren't here?" I asked, my eyebrows raised in question.

"Nah, I worked the day shift on Saturday. It was my oldest son's birthday, so I made sure I was scheduled off. Why do you ask?" He picked up a pen and tapped it on his desktop.

I nudged Candie's foot. "Umm, no reason. I was wondering what the best day of the week is to shop and avoid the Christmas rush for next year. I'm not big on crowds. Claustrophobic, you know." I stood and held out my hand to Howie. "My cousin and I will let you get back to work. We'll be in touch to firm up dates for our book signings. Thanks so much, and have a Merry Christmas." I gathered my purse up from the floor and turned to Candie.

Howie stood and handed each of us his business card. "Been a pleasure, ladies. I look forward to hosting you."

I said goodbye to Ms. Allen as we exited the office, but once again, she was on the phone. After we left the office, I texted my mom to say we were done at the mall office and would meet her and the boys outside the Happy Moose when they finished eating.

"What do you mean you're claustrophobic? When there's a designer purse sale, you're right in the middle of the mob trying to snatch up the best buy," Candie said as we made our way through the holiday shoppers towards the Happy Moose.

"Don't you see? Howie could have murdered Mr. Sayers. He says he was at home celebrating his son's birthday, but was he really? Didn't he look a little nervous when we asked him where he was Saturday night? We only have his word for it. Oops." I stumbled as a woman with her arms lined with shopping bags bumped into me.

"Hmmm, that is possible," Candie said.

"Possible? I'd say more than likely. After all, he said his boys are involved in sports, and at Loopy Ladies, Anita Plum has often mentioned how expensive it is for her twins to be involved in the activities they love. How could Howie's boys enjoy all they do if their dad lost his job because of a Don Juan Santa?"

"Yeah, but if their dad wound up in jail, how would that help the boys' sports career?" Candie asked. She stopped in front of a jewelry store window to admire their display of rings. I wondered if she had one picked out for Santa to leave under her tree.

Candie had knocked the wind out of my theory of Howie being Mr. Sayers's murderer. She was right. Being convicted of murder certainly wouldn't help Howie's sports budget.

Unfortunately, this still left my dad on the suspect list for Mr. Sayers's murder. Hopefully, I could find his murderer soon and the jingling we'd hear was the sound of Santa's sleigh bells and not handcuffs on my dad's wrists.

We continued down the mall towards the men's store for the sweater I wanted to buy Hank for Christmas. "I need to duck in here quickly and buy a present for Hank. I'll only be a minute."

Candie followed me into the store. I wandered the aisles towards the sweater section, where I found what I wanted. I couldn't wait to see Hank wearing the sweater, which matched the crystal blue color of his eyes. He'd look sexier than any man on the cover of Candie's romance novels.

As I walked towards the checkout counter, a large woman whose arms were laden with packages plowed into me. Two of her bags dropped to the floor. After I regained my balance, I bent to help her pick them up, only to be met with a scowl and a nasty, "You should watch where you're going."

I shrugged. It wasn't entirely my fault she had dropped her purchases. She was obviously in a rush and hadn't watched where she was going. As I looked at her, she looked vaguely familiar, but I couldn't put a name to her face. I said, "Sorry" and sent a "Merry Christmas" to her retreating back as she hurried away. I shook my head then proceeded towards the checkout to pay for Hank's sweater.

* * *

After my purchase, I caught up with Candie, who was eyeing a display of men's Christmas socks. "I'm finished," I said, sliding the handles of the bag containing the sweater up my arm. We left the store, and as we rounded a corner, I spied my mom, Eli and Landon sitting on a bench outside the restaurant. I smiled. The two little guys plus my mom sported paper moose antlers on their heads. Upon seeing Candie and me, the boys jumped off the bench and ran towards us.

Eli beat his brother to us and was the first to speak, nudging his brother out of the way. "Sam! Candie! We had the bestest time. Aunt Barbara is so much fun. There was a person dressed as a moose walking around the restaurant. Aunt Barbara took our picture with him."

"Then she said we could have anything we wanted to eat," Landon added, finally able to get a word in. He proceeded to tell us everything they'd eaten. My stomach ached hearing about the hamburger, fries, milk shakes, and cookies they'd consumed. I hoped we wouldn't be sorry later if they developed a stomachache on the ride home. I didn't think Gladys would be happy if the boys christened the pink leopard covering the back seat of her car.

"That all sounds yummy, but how about we head home and see if we can find a Christmas movie on the television?" I asked. My mom looked like she was about to fall asleep on the bench—tired, I was sure, from keeping up with two energetic boys.

"Yeah." The moose antlers bobbled as they jumped up and down.

"I hope *Elf* is on TV," Eli said as we walked towards the mall exit.

"I want to see *Santa Claus,*" Landon replied, jabbing his brother with his elbow.

I hugged Candie goodbye. She was going to spend a little more time at the mall shopping for Mark.

Mom laughed. "It's going to be a lively evening."

We didn't know how lively when I pulled into my drive twenty minutes later.

CHAPTER TWENTY-FIVE

―――――

As we approached our car, I noticed a silver Jaguar parked next to it. I would love to own such a luxurious automobile, but such a dream would have to wait until I won the lotto. "Boys, be careful getting into the car. We don't want to nick the car next to us."

"Yeah," Mom agreed. "A person would probably have to take out a bank loan to pay for any repairs to the car. It certainly is out of my budget."

"Yours and mine both," I said over my shoulder as I buckled Eli into his seat.

With everyone settled and buckled in, I turned in my seat to back out of my parking space. The woman who had bumped into me in the men's store stood behind the Jaguar. I presumed she owned the beautiful car and was making sure I didn't damage it. As I drove past her, I waggled my fingers, only to be rewarded with a scowl. Again, it niggled at the back of my brain that I'd known her from somewhere but couldn't put a name to her face.

The ride home from the mall was filled with the boys' lively conversation about their visit to Santa. They repeated what they'd told him they wanted for Christmas. Eli again said he wanted Matchbox cars, and Landon said Santa was going to bring him a trampoline. I laughed and wondered if Hank's sister knew what was on the boys' list.

I pulled Gladys's car into my driveway and frowned. A black sedan with a dented back fender was parked in front of my garage. Rust dotted the side of the car. Next to it sat a blue SUV.

"The blue car is the Feinsteins' rental, but I wonder who the black car belongs to?" Mom asked.

"I'm afraid I know who owns that heap," I said, wondering why he would be at my house.

Mom unbuckled the boys from their booster seats as I gathered up my package. The guys were eager to show Dad the gifts

Mrs. Claus had given them. With the crayons and coloring books clutched in their hands, they skipped ahead of us to the front door. My ears perked up. Shouting traveled through the door, accompanied by Porkchop barking. Mom turned to me with a questioning look on her face. I shrugged then pushed the door open.

"You slimy slug, get out of this house before I sic my daughter's dog on you!"

Mom hurried forward to the den where the ruckus was coming from. I looked down at the boys, who stared up at me with wide eyes. "Here, sit at the dining room table and color a picture for Uncle Chuck while I see what's going on."

They nodded and settled at the table with their coloring books and crayons.

I marched over to the den door, only to have my back stiffen when I saw who was in there with my dad and mom—Rob Anderson.

What did the snake want with my father? He was never up to any good, and I trusted him as much as I did Porkchop refusing to eat a bowl of his kibble. I strode in the room with my back ramrod straight.

"Rob Anderson… What do you want?"

Dad turned to me. His face was red with anger. I worried that whatever Rob wanted had made his blood pressure zoom up. Rob would be sorry if he caused Dad to have a stroke.

Rob glanced over at me with a sneer on his face. A lock of his stringy hair fell over his forehead. "I was asking your dad and Mr. Feinstein here—" Rob flicked his thumb towards the men in question "—about some information that has come to light concerning the landfill where they used to work."

I turned my attention to my dad. Was Rob referring to what Hank had told me about the landfill?

Dad's shoulders slumped. "It looks like the landfill where Herb and I worked was doing some shady business with a construction company, and this fellow thinks we were in on it."

Mom gasped then swayed. I hurried to her side and put an arm around her waist to steady her. If I didn't think Rob would sue me, I would have punched him in the nose.

My frown deepened. "That's crazy. My dad worked there for over twenty years, and there was never any hint of wrongdoing." I gave my best evil eye to Rob. "You have a lot of nerve coming into my house and accusing my dad and his friend of such nonsense. What proof do you have?"

Rob puffed out his scrawny chest like one of the roosters that had strutted around Memaw Parker's farmyard. "You know I'm an investigative reporter for the *Tribune,* and it has come to my attention a certain construction company was allowed to bury its toxic materials at the landfill in containers not approved by the EPA. Apparently, those drums have deteriorated over the years, and the contents are now polluting the land at the dump and the surrounding area. They could cause a possible health hazard."

If Rob's information was correct, this would be a major scandal, and someone could possibly go to jail. But this was Rob Anderson we were dealing with, and gossip was his middle name. He'd made unsubstantiated claims in his articles in the past, only to have to retract them, but not until after the damage was done to someone's reputation. I wouldn't let Rob's lust for gossip harm my dad or his good friend.

I wasn't about to accept what he told us as the truth. "So, Rob, who is your big snitch in this matter, and why do you think my dad and Mr. Feinstein would know anything about this?"

Rob pointed a finger at my dad. I shivered when I saw the dirt under his fingernail. Yuck. "I was working with another reporter at my newspaper on this case and received information from a source that led us to the findings about the toxic waste buried at the landfill."

A thought clicked in my brain. Hank had mentioned he couldn't tell me what was on Mr. Sayers's laptop. Was Sayers the other reporter Rob worked with? Did he kill Theo so he could claim this article as his own in hopes of winning a Pulitzer Prize? People had killed for less. Maybe they had a big argument over who should take credit for breaking such a bombshell article. It would certainly rock the local communities if this information got out. Rosa did mention Rob had stopped by earlier in the day and the two men had gotten into a heated argument. What if he had returned later in the evening and approached Mr. Sayers after he left my house? Maybe Rob continued with the argument from earlier in the day, snapped, and killed him. This article could really make Rob's newspaper career, especially if he wanted to break into a big city market.

"So, Rob, just what do you think my father and Mr. Feinstein would know about these 'shady dealings' at the landfill?" I asked, shaking my finger in irritation at the sleazy man.

Rob shifted from foot to foot. My direct question must have made him a bit uncomfortable. He probably was used to himself posing the questions and not the other way around.

"Umm…I figured since they worked there for so long, they might know a thing or two about it."

I got nose-to-nose with Rob. I had to hold my breath, as he had a bad case of halitosis. I poked him in the chest with my finger as I spoke. "You mean you thought they'd tell you they were in on the dirty deeds? Well, buddy, you thought wrong. These two men are the most honest, hardworking fellows you will ever meet, and if at the time they knew of such shenanigans, they would have reported them to the proper authorities. *Hmmm*… Which makes me wonder if you are so desperate for this story, you might have killed Mr. Sayers. I wonder if the police are looking into such a possibility?"

Rob's Adam's apple bobbed up and down as I poked my thoughts home. Sweat broke out on his upper lip. Now why would he be so nervous?

"I think I have all the information I need right now for my article," Rob said, pulling a knit cap out of the pocket of his stained coat and shoving it on his head.

"Fine, and make sure my dad's name or Mr. Feinstein's aren't mentioned in it, or you'll hear from our lawyer," I shouted after him as he hurried towards the front door.

I felt an arm slide across my shoulder. I looked up to see a huge grin on my dad's face. "Muffin, I couldn't be prouder of you. You certainly put that fellow in his place."

I nodded. "I knew you two would never be part of such a terrible scheme."

Dad leaned down and kissed the top of my head.

"You're right sweetheart, but someone was, and I wonder if that person killed Theo to keep the story from appearing in the *Tribune*." Mom said, getting up from the loveseat and walking over to me.

CHAPTER TWENTY-SIX

———

"Come on. Let's see what the boys are up to. They have a lot to tell you, Dad, about their visit with Santa," I said, leading the way out of the den.

Mr. Feinstein's phone pinged. He dug it out of his back jeans pocket and read the text he had received. "I'll need to take a rain check. That was Marge. She was visiting with her sister while I was here and is ready for me to pick her up. I'd better get going. We're eating dinner with our daughter and her family." He snatched his coat off a chair that sat in the corner of the room and shrugged into it.

"Okay, Herb. Say hi to her and the rest of your family for us," Mom said, handing him his gloves that sat on the seat of the chair.

"I'm parked behind you, so let me move Gladys's car," I said.

"Don't bother, Muffin. I'll do that," Dad said, holding his hand out for the keys to the car.

We followed Mr. Feinstein out of the room. Mom and Dad proceeded to the front door while I stopped in the dining room to be with the boys.

"Can I see what you're coloring?" I asked, leaning over their shoulders.

Both boys nodded vigorously. Grins spread across their faces.

"I'm coloring Santa and his sleigh," Eli said, holding up his coloring book.

"Mine's better," Landon said, showing me a picture of elves busy painting toys in Santa's workshop.

"Is not," Eli said, pointing to Landon's drawing. "You didn't stay in the lines."

Landon jutted out his small lip. "Is, too."

Mom walked into the room. "Whoa. What's all the fussing about? Santa's watching, you know."

I smiled as both boys' eyes widened at Mom's statement. Obviously, the mention of Santa watching still held great weight with them.

"Would anyone like some hot chocolate and cookies?" Mom asked.

"I do. I do," Eli and Landon said in unison as they bounced on their chairs.

After all they had eaten at the mall, I couldn't imagine them being hungry, but obviously they were growing boys and had what Memaw Parker used to call a "hollow leg." They jumped off their chairs and followed Mom into the kitchen.

I was about to tag along when my phone buzzed. "I'll be right with you," I called out then pulled my phone out of the back pocket of my slacks. I glanced down—Hank. With him so busy with Mr. Sayers's murder I hadn't heard much from him, but that was normal when he was involved with a murder case.

I smiled and swiped my phone. "Hi, Hank. I miss you. How are things going?" rushed out of my mouth.

Hank chuckled. "I miss you, too, Sam. The case is going slowly. But I have another kind of emergency that I was wondering if you could help me with."

I heard yelping in the background that didn't sound like Nina, Hank's dog. "Hank, what's that I hear?"

"That's the problem I need help with," he said, desperation lacing his voice. "Nina, no. Don't do that to Mitzy."

"Mitzy?" I asked.

"Yeah, Mitzy," Hank said then proceeded to tell me about his emergency.

I told him to come right over. He thanked me and said he'd be here in a matter of minutes.

After we hung up, I walked into the kitchen. The boys sat at the kitchen table, happily sipping their hot chocolate and munching on cookies. "Boys, your uncle Hank will be here soon, and he's bringing your dog Mitzy with him.

They jumped off their chairs and hopped up and down, joy written all over their faces. Dad had joined Mom in the kitchen, and they turned to me with puzzled looks on theirs. I took them aside and explained the situation to them.

"Since his sister is on bed rest, she can't watch Mitzy. Hank agreed to take her until her husband gets home from overseas, but apparently Mitzy and Nina don't get along and have been growling at each other since Hank brought her to his house."

"Oh, my, what a problem," Mom said, shaking her head.

"Fingers crossed, I only hope Mitzy and Porkchop fare better," I said, watching the boys hop around my kitchen in excitement at the prospect of having their dog with them. Porkchop yelped at their feet. He probably thought they were playing a game with him.

I heard my front door open. "Sam, I'm here," Hank called from the living room.

True to his word, it had only taken him a few minutes to arrive here. Things must have been pretty desperate for him to drive so fast.

Eli and Landon raced into the living room with Porkchop leading the way. Mom, Dad, and I followed behind. I came to an abrupt halt when I saw a little white puff ball and Porkchop eyeing each other up.

"Hi, Sam. This is Mitzy," Hank said, a pink leash dangling from his fingers. He unhooked what I assumed was a very fluffy Pomeranian, although my knowledge of various breeds of dogs was limited to dachshunds.

I held my breath as the dogs sniffed each other. Porkchop's tail was the first to wag, and then Mitzy's joined in the squirming. Porkchop barked as if conveying a message to the other dog. He turned and raced towards the kitchen with Mitzy following.

"Mitzy!" Eli and Landon shouted and scurried after their dog with smiles spread across their faces.

"How ya' doing, Hank?" my dad asked, pounding Hank on the back.

Hank stumbled a step then righted himself. He was a big guy at a little over six foot, but my dad had at least thirty pounds on him.

My petite mom was gentler with her hug for Hank. "It's so good to see you, Hank. I think that puppy is the perfect medicine for those boys. I know they've been missing their momma."

I hadn't thought of how the boys' separation from their mother must be affecting them. With their father deployed overseas, they may be a bit more used to that situation, but their mom was a constant presence in their lives. Some babysitter I was. Hank was more in tune with the boys' feelings than I was. Watching him interact with them made me realize more and more what a great dad he would have been. Was I robbing him of this opportunity by dating him? Should he be with a younger woman who could give him a child? I shook my head to dispel these disturbing thoughts. They could wait for another day.

"How do you know, Mom? They seemed to be having a good time with us so far," I asked, wondering if I should do more for them.

"While we were having lunch at the Happy Moose, they dropped a few hints about how they missed their mom but were excited their dad would be home soon," Mom said, walking beside me into the kitchen.

I smiled at the sight that greeted us as we entered the room. Eli and Landon sat on the tile floor with Porkchop and Mitzy squirming on their laps.

"Boys, would you like to give the doggies a treat?" I asked, reaching up into the cupboard where I stored Porkchop's goodies.

"Yes, yes," the boys shouted.

They pushed off the floor and scurried over to me with outstretched hands. I placed two Doggie Yummies in their hands. Porkchop and Mitzy sat gazing up at the boys, waiting for the treats to fall their way.

As I watched the boys feed the dogs, it occurred to me that I needed to mention to Hank about Rob Anderson's visit to my house earlier today, and I really should tell him about the flowers and card at Rosa's. "Mom, Dad, could you watch the boys for a few minutes? I want to talk to Hank."

"Sure, Muffin, you take all the time you want. These little fellas are in good hands," Dad said, sneaking two more treats to the guys to hand the dogs.

I raised an eyebrow at Dad, but he shrugged and gave me his most innocent look.

As I led Hank out of the kitchen towards the den, he asked, "So what's brewing under those curly locks of yours?" He ran a playful hand through my hair.

"I believe I have a good lead for you as to who may have killed Mr. Sayers."

CHAPTER TWENTY-SEVEN

Hank stopped before the den door, his strong hand on the brass knob and a frown on his face. "Saaam," he drawled out. "How many times do I have to ask you to keep your pretty little nose out of police business?"

My back stiffened at his comment. "A few times, maybe?"

Hank opened the den door and motioned for me to enter the room before him. We walked over to the loveseat and sat, not exactly close to each other, as the evening's mood had cooled a bit with my grand pronouncement.

Hank ran his fingers through his dark-brown wavy hair. My fingers itched to push back that stubborn lock with a mind of its own that lingered on his forehead. I figured now was not the best moment for such a gesture.

"A few times? How about every murder investigation I've been involved in since leaving Albany and moving to Wings Falls?"

I sat bolt upright. "Hank, that's not fair. You know that all those murders have either involved me or people I care about. I'm not about to stand aside and be sent up the river to be Big Bertha's roomie, nor am I going to let that happen to my friends and now my father and his buddy."

Hank heaved an exasperated sigh. "Sam, I know you're not, but murder can be a dangerous business, and I don't want you getting hurt."

I took one of Hank's calloused hands into mine and raised it to my lips. I placed a soft kiss on the palm. "I appreciate your concern. Believe me I do, but I know my dad and Mr. Feinstein did not murder Mr. Sayers."

"Sam, have some faith in me and the police department, please. I'm working really hard to find the killer and clear your dad's and his friend's names." Hank looked at me with pleading eyes.

I scooted back on the loveseat to put a few inches between us. I had to have a clear head while I related all that Candie and I had learned at the mall today about Mr. Sayers's stint as Santa and the faint possibility that Anita Plum's husband, Tony, could have whacked Theo as retribution for how crude he was with his daughters while they worked at Santa's booth. After all, people were coming and going from my party the other night. What if Tony had slipped out at some point in the night for a breath of fresh air, saw Mr. Sayers on his front lawn, and had it out with him concerning Theo's treatment of his daughters. After doing the deed, he could have snuck back into the house with no one the wiser. I certainly hoped this wasn't what happened, as I liked the couple. I had gotten to know Anita and her family from her amusing tales about life with teenagers at our Monday morning Loopy Lady meetings. But I certainly didn't want my dad and his buddy to be accused of Mr. Sayers's murder, either. Then there was the possibility that maybe Rosa had killed her husband to be with a long-lost love.

I looked into Hank's crystal blue eyes and related all of our findings to him. He sat still, taking in every word I said. "Oh, and I can't forget—the mall manager."

Hank raised an eyebrow at the mention of the manager.

"Yes, he has just as good a reason to have wanted Mr. Sayers out of the picture, too," I said.

A smile quirked Hank's lips. "If he was having problems with Santa, wouldn't it have been less messy to fire him than kill the jolly ole fellow? I doubt the mall hires hitman elves to do away with Santas who don't measure up. Wouldn't it be easier to send Santa back to the North Pole? Maybe assign him to a job on the toy assembly line? That should straighten him out."

I swatted Hank's arm. "I'm serious. Candie and I quizzed the mall manager, and he wasn't happy with Mr. Sayers. He was afraid that Theo's bad behavior might cause trouble for the mall and in turn possibly get him fired if he didn't get rid of Mr. Sayers. The manager mentioned that he has sons involved in sports and has a lot of expenses associated with it."

Now Hank sat up straighter in his chair. Apparently I had piqued his interest with that last bit of news. "How did you and Candie discover all this?"

A grin spread across my face. So now poking my nose in certain places was interesting to him. "Oh, you know my cousin. She can worm her way into anything." I didn't want to mention her little white lie about the two of us wanting book signings at the mall. Then again, maybe they would happen—she with her romance novels and Porkchop and me with his Superhero book.

Mrs. Sayers and her possible lover? Should I mention them? Candie has said that the significant other is often the main suspect in a murder. I hated to do this to Rosa, but my dad's innocence was more important to me, so I told Hank about the flowers and card that went with them.

Hank nodded at this information and said he'd send Officer Greensleeves over to question Mrs. Sayers once again.

Lastly, I needed to tell him about Rob Anderson's visit here a few hours ago. To me, Rob had the most to lose—the article that he claimed Mr. Sayers stole from him and the Pulitzer Prize he could almost wrap his grubby fingers around.

I cleared my throat. "Rob Anderson paid my dad and Mr. Feinstein a visit while Mom, the boys, and I were at the mall this afternoon."

Hank grimaced. It was obvious from the look on his face he was no fan of the reporter, either. "What did that creature want?"

Well, that was putting it bluntly. "He seems to think Dad and Mr. Feinstein are involved in some illegal shenanigan at the landfill where they worked most of their life. He said he had evidence the landfill was involved in a toxic waste coverup and is going to expose it in an article he had written."

Hank shifted in his seat. He looked uncomfortable with what I had related to him.

"Hank, what do you know that you're not telling me? You know my dad and his friend would never do anything illegal."

Hank took my hands in his. "Sam, you have to realize I need to investigate all information that comes to my attention."

"What is this so-called information you have? If it's from the likes of Rob Anderson, it's rubbish." I stared into his eyes and tried to see if I could read his mind, but to no avail.

Hank shook his head. "No, Officer Greensleeves and I have been poring over the documents on Theo Sayers's laptop to see if there is any connection between the information he had gathered on the landfill and his murder."

"So, he was working on the article, too. Doesn't that prove that Rob had a reason to kill Mr. Sayers? You know Rob can practically taste that Pulitzer."

Hank shook his head. "Rob says he was covering a Christmas parade over in Sandy Hill at the time Theo was murdered."

I pulled my hands out of his and wrapped my arms around my body to ward off the chill that gripped me after hearing Hank's words. I stood and started to pace the den. "Hank, what are you talking about? Do you believe him? Sandy Hill is the town next to us. Rob could have killed Mr. Sayers and driven there in less than ten minutes. You know my dad and Mr. Feinstein would never do anything illegal." My anger at Rob Anderson grew by the second. How could that slime ball accuse such a good person as my dad of such a terrible thing?

Hank's phone pinged. He'd received a text, and I was sure it was from the station. He slipped his phone out of the inside pocket of his coat and glanced at it. "It's work," he said, scrolling down the phone's screen.

I calmed down enough to sit next to him on the loveseat. "I figured as much. I guess you must go back to the station?" Now I was angry with Rob Anderson for cutting my evening with Hank short. To say the least, I was not in a good mood.

Hank read his phone message again then looked at me. "Do you know a Laurine Bateman?"

CHAPTER TWENTY-EIGHT

I scanned my memory to recall if I knew such a person and came up blank. "I'm sorry, Hank, I can't say I do, and Wings Falls being a small town, I know almost everyone."

Hank leaned towards me and brushed a stray curl behind my ear. He stood and held out a hand to help me off the loveseat then gathered me into his arms and kissed me. When we parted for air, he said, "That's okay. As you said, you know almost everyone in town, and I was hoping you might have heard of her."

"Is she someone important?" I asked, tracing a finger down the front of his coat.

"That's what we don't know yet. Her name popped up once on Theo's laptop, so we're trying to contact everyone he's mentioned."

"Sorry I can't help," I said. Was her name mentioned in Mr. Sayers's article?

Hank laughed. "I shouldn't be asking you anyway. Joe Peters has lived here as long as you, so I'll run the name by him."

"I understand Mimi Greensleeves has been putting him through his paces."

A chuckle escaped Hank. "Yeah, the station commander wants the guys to shape up, and Joe isn't very happy about that. How'd you know about Joe?"

"Candie and I ran into Mimi at Sweetie Pie's. Joe happened to limp in after her, so I asked her about him. I guess she's really giving him a workout at Fitness World."

"Oh, I'm sure you were filled with concern about Joe's condition," Hank said. Laughter filled his voice.

I put on my most innocent look. "Of course I was. It is the Christmas season after all and time for good will towards all."

Hank shook his head. "Yeah, and I have a bridge in Brooklyn to sell you."

I playfully punched his arm. "Well, maybe I did gloat a little bit."

"A little bit?" Hank asked then pulled me into his arms for one last kiss before he had to leave for the police station.

"Look, look. Uncle Hank is kissing Sam," two voices shouted from the den door.

I jumped back from Hank's arms. Red flushed my cheeks as I looked over at Eli and Landon.

"Are you going to get married?" Eli asked.

My mouth fell open, and I started to stammer. "Ummm, no. No, we're not."

Hank walked towards the boys and knelt before them. "Would you fellows like Sam as your aunt?"

My eyes widened. What was he saying to these boys? "Hank, shouldn't you be getting over to the police station?"

He looked up at me from his position in front of his nephews. He pushed off his knees and stood. A grin spread across his face. "Okay, I'll be on my way," he said, ruffling the boys' hair. He walked over to me and leaned closer. "This is a conversation to be continued," he whispered for only me to hear.

"Go on, get to work and find my neighbor's killer," I said, giving him a playful push towards the den door.

"I'll send Officer Greensleeves over to question Mrs. Sayers further about the information you gave me." He laughed all the way to the front door.

Moments later, Mom and Dad walked into the den. "Hank's left already? I was going to throw a pizza in the oven," Mom said.

"Yeah, I wanted to ask him if he's got any new leads on who did Theo in," Dad said.

"Chuck, hush," Mom said, cocking her head towards Eli and Landon.

"Oh yeah, right," Dad said.

"He got a text from work and needed to get back," I said.

"We saw Uncle Hank kissing Sam," Landon said.

I rolled my eyes towards the ceiling. I was fast finding out that nothing was quiet around youngsters.

"Oh, he kissed her, huh?" Dad asked. "Should I have him arrested?"

Eli and Landon giggled at my dad's suggestion of arresting their uncle.

I heaved a sigh. "Dad…don't encourage the boys." Leave it up to him to egg the boys on. I needed to stop this conversation right away before it started. The clock hanging on the wall next to the fireplace in the living room chimed nine times. I blinked, surprised that the evening had flown by so fast. Exhaustion filled my body. I could fall asleep right now and not wake up until noon tomorrow, but I needed to wrangle the boys into bed and see to the dogs.

In perfect timing, Landon scrubbed his eyes, and Eli let out a loud yawn. I had a feeling that when I mentioned bedtime, I wouldn't get much resistance from either of them.

"Fellows, how about hitting the sack? It's been a long day, and I'm really tired." I glanced across the room and saw Mitzy and Porkchop curled up under my desk next to each other, sound asleep. Mitzy was snoring in a most unladylike manner for such a small critter.

Eli turned his small face up to me. "Can Mitzy sleep with us? She does at home."

"Puh-leease," Landon joined in his brother's plea.

My heart melted as I looked into their sweet faces. "Sure."

The boys jumped for joy at the thought of sharing their bed with Mitzy.

"Say, fellas, how about if we take a swing by your house tomorrow and check on your momma?" my dad asked.

Eli and Landon let out an ear-piercing shriek. They'd been very good about giving their mother the rest she needed, but I knew they missed her terribly. Mom and Dad had entertained them with stories and coloring, but it didn't make up for being with their mother. Mom had let them phone their mother to check in, but we kept those calls to a minimum to give Hank's sister the rest she needed.

I glanced at the boys hopping around my den in excitement. Both Mitzy and Porkchop had joined in the commotion, barking and prancing at the boys' feet. "Dad, can you handle all of this energy?"

He pasted a wounded look on his face. "What are you talking about? We're men and stick together. Right, guys? We'll make a morning of it and have breakfast at the Pancake Palace. How does that sound? I hear they make the best banana pancakes in town."

"Yummy!" both boys shouted in unison.

Mom and I laughed. "Okay, I'll text Hank and let him know your plans so he can tell his sister, Amelia, and his mother you are coming," I said. "Mom, while they're doing their man thing, why don't we stop by Sweetie Pie's for a bite to eat?" I grabbed my phone from the top of my desk where I had placed it when Hank and I were in the room earlier and shot Hank a message informing him my dad and the boys were going to see their mom. He answered almost immediately. I smiled at the smiley face emoji and the *I love you!* he sent in return.

"Okay, guys. You don't want to fall asleep in your banana pancakes tomorrow morning, so let's hurry off to bed. Here, grab on to my legs, and I'll give you a lift to your bedroom."

Mom and I laughed out loud as Dad dragged the boys down the hallway clinging to his legs. Porkchop and Mitzy followed behind, barking and wagging their tails.

* * *

"I don't know who was more excited about going to Pancake Palace this morning, Dad or the boys," I said as I pulled into Sweetie Pie's parking lot. "Oh, I see Candie beat us here."

I had called her earlier to see if she wanted to meet Mom and me at the café for breakfast. Her answer was an emphatic yes. Mark was busy working, so she was free. I pulled the Bug into a slot next to Precious.

As Mom and I walked towards the restaurant's entrance, I spotted a silver Jaguar parked next to the door. As I had at the mall, I wondered who in Wings Falls would own such an expensive car.

CHAPTER TWENTY-NINE

———

A blast of welcome warm air greeted us as we entered Sweetie Pie's. "Oh, it's just like I remembered it when your father and I ate here last year. I miss the fifties vibe Franny has here. No one near us in Florida has anything like it. The atmosphere is so fun and welcoming."

I had to agree with my mother. When Franny Goodway opened her restaurant over fifteen years ago, after she'd moved north from Alabama, she decorated it as if we'd just stepped out of an episode of *Happy Days.* As usual, the place was bustling with a breakfast crowd. Spoons clinked against thick porcelain mugs, and music played from the juke boxes situated at the end of each table. I scanned the café and waved to the diners I knew, which was practically everyone. If you didn't look too closely, you wouldn't notice the duct tape on a few of the benches or your meals were served on mismatched dinnerware. That was all part of Sweetie Pie's charm, the thing Franny's restaurant was known for, and that included good food, cleanliness, and its welcoming atmosphere. That more than made up for any worn edges.

"Sam. Over here," I heard as I walked farther into the diner. Candie sat in our favorite booth situated next to a window looking out onto Main Street, where we could people watch—a favorite activity of ours after attending Sunday Mass at Saint Anthony's.

On our way to the booth, I waved to Aaron and Joy through the kitchen pass-through window. They both nodded, too busy preparing the customers' meals to do more than that for Mom and me.

"Hi, Candie," Mom said, slipping off her coat and sliding into the booth.

I hung my down coat on the hook at the end of the booth next to Mom's then took the seat beside her as I glanced around the crowded restaurant. From the smiles and the sound of laughter echoing around the room, the holiday cheer had definitely infected everyone. "This place is hopping."

Candie nodded. A strand of her auburn hair had escaped her violet knit hat and floated about her face. "Yes, thank heavens I got here early, or we wouldn't be able to get our favorite booth."

"How's Mark? Is he working today?" Mom asked, tucking her gloves into her purse.

"I'm afraid so. He was supposed to be off this week, but a pipe broke down at city hall, so he went in to see about the damage." Candie plucked the menus from the slot attached to the metal napkin holder. She placed one in front of herself and handed one each to my mom and me.

I chuckled. "Don't you think we have this memorized by now?" I asked, pointing my menu towards her.

"Yes, but I didn't want Aunt Barbara to think we were hurrying her. Plus, maybe Franny has added something new to the menu since we last ate here. After all, we haven't been here since after church on Sunday."

Mom and I laughed at Candie's statement. "True, true," I said, flipping open my menu. "Since then, she could have completely revamped her offerings. You know, eliminated her crowd pleasers, like her banana cream pie or the yummy cinnamon buns she bakes up every day."

My cousin's eye grew large and one of her ring-filled hands flew to her rhinestone-studded blouse. "Heaven forbid. Don't even say such a thing."

"What's got Candie about to have a fainting spell?"

Our heads swiveled to see Gladys O'Malley standing next to our booth.

"Hi, Gladys." I peered behind her to see if Frank was with her. "Frank's not with you?"

"No, he dropped me off. My Pookie Bear is out doing some last-minute Christmas shopping for his sweetums. I hinted last night that I saw a negligee on sale at The Clothes Horse yesterday when I was shopping in town. I thought he'd love it as much as me."

Oh, how I wanted to scrub the image of her modeling a sexy nightgown for Frank from my mind, but instead I pasted a smile on my face and asked, "Since you're by yourself, would you like to join us for breakfast?"

Gladys beamed at my suggestion. "I'd love it," she said, pulling a wool knit scarf off her green- and red-dyed curls. They sprang back as if they were a Slinky. But she kept on her worn wool coat and slid into the booth next to Candie. "Can you hand me one of those menus, please?" she asked, holding out a gnarled hand to my cousin.

"Aaron fries up a mean batch of ham and eggs. I highly recommend them," Candie said, mentioning Hank's brother and passing her a menu.

"That would hit the spot, and add one of those giant cinnamon rolls, too," Gladys said, slapping the menu closed on the table in front of her.

"Morning, ladies. Are you ready to order?"

I looked over to see Franny standing next to our table with a coffee pot in each hand, regular and decaf. She knew I'd want the one in the orange-banded pot.

We all nodded and held out our mugs to her. As usual, I was the only one ordering what Candie called my "sissy brew." It wasn't my fault my divorce from George had caused my blood pressure to climb and my doctor to relegate me to decaf. Finding out your husband was doing the bump fuzzies with the secretary of the business you co-own would do that.

After serving us coffee, Franny pulled her order pad from the short apron tied around her slim waist. With her pen poised over the pad, she wrote down our orders. For Candie, ham and eggs, and for Gladys the same but with a giant cinnamon roll on the side. Mom surprised me with the exact same order as Gladys. Finally, Franny jotted down my very dull order of a bowl of grits with a pat of butter on top and my big splurge—a side of bacon.

"So, Sam, what did that nephew of mine have to say about Theo Sayers's murder?" Gladys and Hank's mom were sisters. Since I dated her nephew, she often thought she should be privy to Hank's and my conversations.

I peered over the top of my mug of coffee. "Nothing."

"What do you mean nothing? He has to have whispered something into your ear last night?" Gladys said while stirring ten packets of sugar into her coffee. My teeth ached watching all that sweetness dissolve into her coffee.

Heat crawled up my neck. I only wished that my love life was as hopping as hers, but with my parents visiting, Hank and I hadn't had very much alone time and now with Mr. Sayers's murder, it was even more limited. "As usual when he's involved with a murder, he's busy at the police station." I fiddled with the spoon lying next to my coffee mug.

"Well, all I can say from living two doors down from him is that Theo Sayers was a nasty man. Don't you agree, Barbara?" Gladys pointed her spoon at Mom.

Mom shrugged and stared into her mug. "I hate to speak ill of the dead, but he wasn't the nicest person on our street."

Was there something my mom wasn't saying about her dealings with Mr. Sayers? It had always niggled at me that there may have been more than an unrequited teenage crush between them. It couldn't have been more serious than that, could it? I shivered. Certainly not something that made my dad so angry he wanted to kill him, would it?

"Not the nicest person!" Gladys screeched. The veins in her scrawny neck bulged out. "He was a downright evil person. Why, a few years ago, I was going door to door taking up a collection for the American Heart Association. When I knocked on their door, Rosa answered with tears streaming down her face. She had a big nasty purple bruise on the upper part of her arm."

Mom, ever the peacemaker, said, "Maybe she tripped and fell on her way to answer the door."

Gladys heaved out a breath of air. "Barbara, please. The bruise was in the shape of a handprint with finger marks wrapping around her arm. I have no doubt that Theo had inflicted the bruise on her."

I was just as shocked as my mother. True, we didn't have much contact with the Sayers, but I never suspected him of abusing her.

Candie's jaw was set in a hard line. "That egg-sucking dog. I wouldn't have blamed her if she's the one who did him in. If any man ever raised a hand to me, I'd make sure he only sang the high notes for the rest of his life."

As serious as this conversation was, I had to smile at Candie's comment. She certainly knew how to put things in perspective.

"Didn't you ever notice Rosa wearing long sleeves in the summertime—on some of the hottest days, even?" Gladys asked.

Mom placed her coffee mug back on the table and shook her head. "Now that you mention it, I did, but I thought she was one of those people who are cold all the time. I'm sorry I wasn't aware of Theo mistreating her. Maybe I could have been of some help."

"Mom, now don't go blaming yourself for something you knew nothing about. I do wonder, though, could something have happened Saturday night that finally made her snap and she killed Mr. Sayers?" I asked and glanced around the table at the ladies sitting with me.

CHAPTER THIRTY

Candie nodded at my question. "That's certainly possible. Maybe the note we found with the roses was from a long-lost love and she saw him as a way out of her marriage. She is definitely on our list of possible suspects."

Gladys bounced in her seat and rubbed her hands together with glee. "You have a list of suspects who could have bumped off Theo? Tell me, tell me." She waggled her fingers at me.

I thought she was going to burst with excitement. "Well, I guess we can add Rosa Sayers to the top of the list, and then there's Howie the mall manager. He's afraid of losing his job because of Mr. Sayers's un-Santa-like behavior. The husband of one of the moms visiting Santa with her child was upset because Mr. Sayers hit on his wife. I hate to mention it, but Anita Plum said her husband wanted to wring Mr. Sayers's neck for making crude comments to their daughters, who work as Santa's elves at the mall. And I'd put Rob Anderson right up there with Rosa for having a motive for wanting Mr. Sayers out of the picture."

Gladys's gray eyebrows rose up her forehead. "You mean that poor excuse of a reporter who works for the *Tribune*?"

"Yeah, the one and the same." I explained to her about the article concerning the landfill he said Mr. Sayers stole from him and how I thought he counted on it as his ticket to winning the Pulitzer.

Gladys choked on a mouthful of coffee as she laughed out loud. "In that fool's dreams. He's lucky if the editor doesn't put him in charge of writing the lonely hearts column."

I could only wish, but I didn't discount him for wanting Mr. Sayers out of the picture. He'd certainly benefit from his rival's death.

Gladys reached over and pulled a paper napkin out of the metal dispenser at the end of the table and dabbed at the spot of coffee she'd spewed on the front of her oversized sweater. "That's certainly some list of suspects you have there."

I agreed but wasn't going to pile my dad's name or Mr. Feinstein's on the list. No matter how mad my dad and his friend were Saturday night with Mr. Sayers, I knew they couldn't have killed my neighbor, and I wasn't going to bring any suspicion their way.

"Here you go, ladies. You want to scooch back so I can place your meals in front of you?"

I glanced over to see Franny with a large tray balanced on her shoulder. How she handled such a load was beyond me. I knew if I tried, the plates and their contents would end up decorating the tile floor.

We all did as Franny asked as she slid heaping servings of our orders onto the Formica tabletop. My stomach grumbled in anticipation of what I was about to send its way. True, I wasn't going to enjoy one of Franny's famous cinnamon buns, but my mouth watered for my steaming bowl of grits and plate of bacon.

"Hey, waitress. My coffee is cold. I want a refill."

My head snapped around to see who the rude and demanding customer was. I recognized the same woman I'd bumped into at the mall when I was shopping for Hank's Christmas present.

Franny frowned but plastered on a smile. "I'd better see what the diva wants," she said and walked over to the woman's table.

"Mom, who's that person who called to Franny? She looks familiar, but I can't place her," I asked. I tried to pull the memory of her as someone from my past from the back reaches of my brain but couldn't quite do it.

Mom twisted in her seat to see who I was referring to. She squinted at the woman then turned back to the table. "I believe that's Laurine Connors and her parents. You remember her, don't you? Her father owns the landfill where your dad worked."

I shook my head. "Afraid I don't. She was about five years older than me, right?"

Mom nodded. "Yes, that's true, and I guess you really didn't have anything to do with her since they sent her to a private school."

"Was she too good to mingle with the common people?" Candie asked, sliding eggs onto her fork.

"You might say so. Your Uncle Chuck was just one of his employees, so we hardly socialized together. But he got paid well, so it didn't bother him. From what I heard, after high school Laurine went off to some exclusive college then married a successful businessman."

"So, what is she doing back in Wings Falls? Probably thinks she's slumming." I couldn't help my snide comment, not after how she'd spoken to Franny.

"When your father stopped in at Maxwell's Pub the other night, he heard that Mr. Connors isn't in very good health, and from the looks of him sitting at the table, I'd say the rumors are true. I suppose she's home to see him."

I had to agree with Mom's assessment of the frail-looking man huddled in the booth across from Laurine. If anyone appeared to have "one foot in the grave," it was Mr. Connors.

"Mom, Hank mentioned a Laurine Bateman to me. Do you think she's the same person?" I asked.

Mom shrugged. "It could be. I don't know her married name, but Laurine is a tad unusual."

"Well, that certainly hit the spot," Gladys said, rubbing her stomach. Where she'd put all the food she'd eaten, I could only guess. For someone so thin, she had a hearty appetite.

"Ladies, do you care for a top off?" Franny stood at the end of our table gripping coffee pots in her strong hands.

I shook my head. I couldn't manage another swallow of food or drink. "Thank you, Franny, but I'm stuffed." I nodded towards the table where the Connors still sat, engaged in a lively conversation over the morning's newspaper. "You have to put up with a lot as Sweetie Pie's owner."

Franny shrugged her slim shoulders in reply. How she didn't gain weight being around all her fabulous cooking was a mystery to me. If it were me, I'd be joining Mimi Greensleeves' exercise class at Fitness World. I rolled my eyes at the thought of doing jumping jacks next to Joe Peters. "It's all a part of the business. Those type of people are just a fly that I have to flick away."

"I'd be squishing them flat as a pancake if they talked to me that way," Candie said, holding her mug out to Franny for a refill. My cousin was never one to refuse a shot of caffeine.

"What's got them buried in this morning's paper? Did a major story break in Wings Falls over night that we're not aware of?" I asked.

Franny set the coffee pots on the edge of the table then scanned the café to see if anyone was listening to us. "That reporter,

Rob Anderson, has written an article about the landfill. It says the landfill was involved in some shady dealings with a local contractor. I haven't had time to sit down and read the article. As you can see, we've been busy this morning, but the headlines were pretty damning of the landfill."

From the packed tables, I could understand why Franny hadn't had a free moment to herself. "You don't happen to have a spare issue of the paper behind the counter, do you?" I asked Franny. The *Tribune* usually dropped off a couple of freebie copies of the morning edition at the restaurant to help build its readership.

"Wait one second. I might. Let me see if the copy I tucked back behind the counter is still there." Franny grabbed up the coffee pots and darted behind the counter that faced the kitchen pass-through. She held up a newspaper and waved it at us.

"Here you go, ladies," Franny said, returning to our table with the paper tucked under her arm and the coffee pots in her hands. "Enjoy. I'd better get back to my customers, but let me top the rest of you off before I go."

I changed my mind and held my mug out with the rest of the ladies. I needed to fortify myself before reading what Rob Anderson had written.

"Here, let me read what that rascal has to say," Gladys said, snatching the paper off the table and laying it out in front of her. "Blackmail, hazardous waste, polluting the land. That's really serious stuff."

"Woo-wee. Those are some accusations he's throwing against the landfill owner," Candie said, her bejeweled fingers wrapped around her coffee mug.

"You can say that again," Gladys said. She poked a gnarled finger at the paper. "The owner says it's all lies and he can prove it."

CHAPTER THIRTY-ONE

―――

"At least Rob doesn't accuse anyone else in the landfill owners' shenanigans," Mom said.

Was that a look of relief I saw on her face? Did she know more than what was written in this article? "Mom, when Dad worked for Mr. Connors, did he ever mention anything about what Rob says was going on at the landfill?"

Mom shook her head. "No, never. You know he wouldn't have put up with such nonsense. He'd have reported it to the proper authorities right away if he suspected anything like that going on."

I smiled. That was my dad for you—straight as an arrow. He'd have quit first before being a part of anything shady. "I see this is a two-part article and more is to come in tomorrow's morning edition. I wonder what else Anderson has on Mr. Connors." I glanced over to the table where he and his family sat. They seemed far from happy as they read what I assumed was the same article.

I jerked my head towards their table. "Their daughter certainly doesn't look happy. You say she moved away from Wings Falls after high school, Mom?"

Mom nodded. "Yes, she always seemed embarrassed that her father made his living owning a landfill. Like I mentioned before, her parents sent her to private schools, and she moved away after high school to attend a college closer to New York City."

"Hmmm, sounds like she was mighty highfalutin. As Memaw Parker would say, 'She's so stuck up, she thinks the sun comes up just to hear her crow.'"

Laughter circled the table. "Candie, I'd say you are spot on with that assessment," I said. "It looks like she did all right for herself, judging by the designer coat and purse she has in the booth with her." A Louis Vuitton was on my wish list for my designer purse collection. "Didn't you say she married well, too?"

Mom nodded. "Yes, but I think Marge said she's divorced now."

I laughed. "You and your friend have been up from Florida only a few days but have been able to catch up on all the local gossip?"

Mom shrugged. "What can I say? People love to spread news about other's misfortunes."

That was so true. When George and I were going through our divorce, I was sure we were a hot topic on the Wings Falls gossip line.

Candie tucked her napkin next to her plate and slid out of the booth.

"Where are you going?" I asked.

"I need to make a trip to the ladies' room. Maybe on the way, I'll check out the article Gladys read us. Come on. Let's see what this Laurine has to say about what Rob Anderson wrote."

Candie wasn't about to beat around the bush. She was on a mission and ready to get to the root of the matter.

Mom and Gladys watched as I shrugged and slipped out of the booth right behind Candie. Since I hadn't seen Laurine in years and hadn't had any real contact with her while I was growing up, I was trying to think of what I'd say to her.

"We're going to sue the *Tribune* and this hack reporter Rob Anderson. He won't get away with printing these lies." An angry Laurine jabbed at the newspaper spread across the table in front of her. Her long black hair bobbed against shoulders that shook with rage.

"Hi, Laurine and Mr. and Mrs. Connors. It's been a ton of years since I've seen you," I said, stopping beside their table.

Laurine sniffed and looked down her nose at Candie and me. "Do I know you two?"

"I'm Samantha Reynolds Davies, and this is my cousin, Candie Parker-Hogan. We were enjoying breakfast with my mom and friends, and I happened to notice you doing the same with your parents. Thought I'd stop by and say hi," I said. It almost scared me how easily the lies slid off my tongue—almost.

"Whatever," Laurine said, turning her attention back to the *Tribune* article.

"Well, Samantha. It's been a good many years since I've seen you," Mrs. Connors said, ignoring her daughter.

Mrs. Connors and her husband were a few years older than my parents. Her face was lined with wrinkles, and her hair was a silver gray. She sat on the bench seat next to her husband. He sat huddled into his coat, hunched over a plate of waffles. The Mr. Connors that I remembered of my youth had long ago lost most of his hair.

"What do you two want?" Laurine asked, barely looking up at us.

Manners certainly weren't her long suit.

"Laurine. Please. Watch your manners," her mother admonished, shaking her head.

"Mother, we don't have time for idle chit chat," Laurine said, acting as if we were no more than a pesky fly.

"That is quite an article in this morning's newspaper," Candie said, pointing at the newspaper on the table.

"Lies, all lies. That's what it is," Laurine ground out between clenched teeth.

"It does make some broad accusations," I said.

"Well, my dad wasn't involved in this nonsense," Laurine said, glaring at us.

"If you say so," I said.

"Yes, I do. If I recall, your dad and his friend were dealing with that construction company. I'd bet they were directly involved with the Ferguson Construction Company."

My mouth dropped open at Laurine's comment. She was accusing my dad of being behind the shady dealings of the construction company and the landfill.

Candie jumped in to speak before I could comment. "Sugar, my uncle Chuck would do no such thing. He's as honest a man as you'll ever find."

Laurine's mother reached across the table and patted her daughter's hand. "Now dear, let's calm down. We'll talk to our lawyer and settle all this."

Laurine folded the newspaper and tossed it on the bench next to her. "Whatever you say, Mother. But these two busybodies better not accuse us of anything." With that, she ignored us and returned to sipping her coffee.

I took that as the hint we were being dismissed as the lowly peasants she felt we were and nudged Candie. I lifted my chin towards our booth as a suggestion we should return. Candie got the hint, and we walked back to our booth and slid in.

Gladys turned to us. "So, what did that stuck-up snob have to say?"

I smiled. She certainly didn't mince words.

"Of course she denies all the charges Rob Anderson laid out in his article against the landfill," I said, taking a sip of my cold coffee.

"Darn tootin' she would. Do you think she's going to admit her dad was doing something underhanded?" Gladys said, taking a sip of the prune juice she'd ordered while we were visiting the Connors' table. She swore a glass a day kept her plumbing working. To me it was TMI.

"Mom, did you ever hear any rumors when Dad was working at the landfill about Mr. Connors cutting any deal with the Ferguson Construction Company?"

Mom shook her head. "No, never. You know your dad would never have put up with that nonsense. Neither would Herb Feinstein."

"You're right. Dad and Mr. Feinstein would have quit first." I noticed Franny serving the table next to us and waved to get her attention.

Candie stopped in the process of swiping a coat of her Passion Pink lipstick on her lips. "You can't tell me you're still hungry?"

I laughed. "No. I thought I'd stop by the station on the way home with one of Franny's cinnamon rolls for Hank."

CHAPTER THIRTY-TWO

"Mom, was the landfill a very successful business for Mr. Connors when Dad worked there?" We were back in my Bug with a paper bag containing Franny's cinnamon bun nestled in the back seat.

"I imagine so. At any one time, he had at least eight full-time employees, your dad and Herb being two of them. I never knew his wife to have a job outside of the home. And as you know, Laurine went to the best schools. That was more her mother's doing than her father's. Mrs. Connors always had an air about her. She never socialized with any of her husband's employees."

"When Candie and I walked up to their booth, I noticed Laurine wore a very expensive designer coat. It looked like a Burberry I saw in a fashion magazine, and her purse was a Louis Vuitton. Both of those run in the thousands of dollars. I'll bet her shoes were designer, too, although I'm not familiar with shoe designers." My specialty, if you could count it as one, was designer purses. I was usually first in line when the Clothes Horse, a favorite clothing store on Main Street, ran their annual handbag sale, although my budget was more on the lower end of the designer purse scale. I was an aficionado of scratch and dent offerings.

I pulled into the parking lot of the single-story cinder block building that housed the Wings Falls Police Station. I parked next to a black and white cruiser and swiveled in my seat towards Mom. "Would you like to come in while I deliver the cinnamon bun to Hank?"

She shook her head. "No, while you were visiting the Connors' table, your dad called and said that when he went to leave Hank's sister's place, the boys had such a meltdown that his mom is going to keep them tonight so they can be with their mother. I'm going to touch base with Marge and see if she and Herb would like to go out for a pizza tonight."

"What? You don't want to spend the evening with me?" I asked, opening my door.

"Hon, you've had plenty of Mom and Dad time. I'm sure you'd like to have a few hours with Hank."

True, our alone time had been limited, but that wasn't their fault. As was becoming the norm for us, a murder investigation was butting into our love life. I reached over and gave her a hug. "You're the best. You know that! I couldn't have asked for more perfect parents. Since his nephews are going to spend the night at home, I'll see if Hank is free tonight, and maybe we can have a pizza night ourselves."

Mom swatted at my arm. "You go on now and see if you can arrange that. I'll see what Marge and Herb are up to."

I laughed and reached into the back seat for the bag containing the cinnamon bun I'd bought Hank. As I walked up the sidewalk to the station, Officers March and Reed exited through the brown metal door leading into the reception area of the building. They nodded and responded to my greeting with a tip of their hats and a respectful, "Ma'am."

After I entered the building, I walked over to the desk situated behind bulletproof glass. "Hi, Wanda," I said to the PCO— the Public Communications Officer—who sat at a desk.

Wanda Thurston's dark skin was a sharp contrast to the bright smile that greeted me in return. "Sam, how are you doing? I haven't seen you in a while."

Since dating Hank, I'd become a familiar person around the station. I often visited him in his office and brought a goodie to eat, as I was doing now with the cinnamon bun. "Busy with Christmas," I replied to her question, speaking into the small hole cut into the thick glass that separated us.

She nodded. Her tight black curls hugged the headphones circling her head.

"Is Hank free?"

"He has someone in with him at the moment, but they've been there for a while. I'll buzz and let him know you're here." Wanda reached over to flip up a switch on the console in front of her.

"Oh, no," I said, raising my hand. "I don't want to interrupt anything."

"Hush, let me check." Wanda spoke into the mouthpiece in front of her.

I couldn't make out what she was saying, but from the smile on her face and nod in my direction, I was about to be let into the inner sanctum of the station. I glanced around the reception area, at its stark brown tile floor, cinder block walls, and the pictures of the station's chief and the state's governor. I smiled. I often wondered what the station would look like if a decorator took it under their wing. Better yet, if Candie applied some of her bling to it.

"Hank says to come on back. He's finished with the person he was interviewing."

"Thanks, Wanda. If I don't see you beforehand, have a great Christmas."

Wanda laughed. She was a single mother with three teenage boys. Her husband had been a Wings Falls Police officer but had been killed in the line of duty. She was doing a great job raising her sons on her own. "Oh, it will be lively, that's for sure. They're getting video games for Christmas, so I imagine it will be video game wars at my house."

The lock on the door leading to the inner working of the station buzzed, letting me know I could enter. I waved to Wanda and walked through the door. I was distracted by the activity going on around me as I passed through the room and didn't notice the person who bumped into me.

"Oh, sorry," I said. "I wasn't watching where I was going." I realized it was Anita Plum's husband as he stepped back from me.

"It's Sam, right?"

I nodded. "Yes. You and Anita were at my house on Saturday night for our Loopy Ladies' Christmas party." I may know all the Loopy Ladies, but the husbands were another story. We usually only got acquainted with them through the occasional picnic or party we'd throw that would include spouses. "Hi, Tony."

"Yep, that's me. Funny running into you here."

"Oh, my boyfriend is a detective on the Wings Falls force. I'm just dropping in to say hi and bring him a goodie from Sweetie Pie's." I held up the bag containing the cinnamon roll. "He was at the party Saturday night. Didn't you meet him?"

Tony frowned and shook his head. "No, I didn't, but I certainly made his acquaintance this morning. I've got to get going. I've wasted enough time here." He pushed past me and out the door leading to the lobby.

I stared after his retreating back. *Now, that was a strange conversation.* I shrugged and continued on to Hank's office, but not before I encountered my nemesis, Joe Peters. He had gotten up from his desk and walked over to the small breakroom that was situated at the back of the room. It contained a counter holding a much used and stained coffeepot, a microwave, and an apartment-sized refrigerator. A devil sitting on my shoulder nudged me forward.

I peeked in the room and spied him pouring a mug of coffee. Next, he loaded a spoon with sugar and stirred it into the coffee. He reached into an open box of powdered doughnuts sitting on the counter and pulled one out. White powder sprinkled onto his black clip-on tie.

"Better not let Mimi Greensleeves see you eating that doughnut, or she'll have you doing extra pushups."

Joe spun around and faced me. Coffee splashed out of his mug and down the front of his shirt and tie. His doughnut crumbled in his fingers and landed on the tip of his shiny black shoes.

If I wasn't mistaken, he uttered a few words under his breath that would even make Memaw Parker blush.

"Are you talking about your family tree?" I asked to egg him on. It was Christmas time, and I should be a bit more charitable, shouldn't I? Nah, not with our history and the multiple times he'd tried to lock me or one of my loved ones up for murder and throw away the key.

"Sam, did you want to see me?"

I turned to see Hank leaning against the door jamb of the breakroom. His arms were folded over his chest. A smirk sat on his face as if he knew what I was up to—trying to needle Joe Peters. "Wanda buzzed to say you were on your way back to see me."

I held up the paper bag I clenched in my hand. "Got a present for you. Grab a cup of coffee to drink with it."

Hank did as I asked and walked over to the coffeepot. He said hello to Joe, who grunted in return. Joe grabbed another doughnut from the box and his coffee then left the room. The coffee splatter and doughnut still lay on the floor. Since I was the cause of the mishap, I felt guilty enough to clean it up in his wake.

Hank poured himself a mug of coffee. He held out the coffeepot towards me, motioning if I wanted a mug, too. I shook my head.

"You know, you really should go easier on Joe. He is a good cop."

I walked over to the trash can and tossed in the paper towels I'd used to clean up Joe's mess then turned to Hank. "I'll become his BFF when he stops trying to fit me with an orange jumpsuit and having Big Bertha become my roomie."

A smile curved Hank's lips. "In other words, not in this lifetime."

"You might say that. Come on. Let's go into your office so you can enjoy what I brought you from Franny's." I hooked my arm through his and led him out of the breakroom to his office.

Once inside his starkly furnished office, I sat on a metal chair across from his desk. Like the lobby, it contained only the essentials—a metal filing cabinet, a scratched metal desk, a picture of the governor on the wall to my right, a bookcase with a wilted plant on the top to my left, and a cushier swivel chair Hank had brought with him when he joined the Wings Falls force behind the desk.

"Hmmm, this looks delicious," Hank said, sliding the cinnamon bun out of the bag. "Want half?" He held the roll towards me.

"No, I'm full. I just finished breakfast and couldn't fit another bite in me. That's all for you to enjoy." Although, I couldn't say I wasn't the tiniest bit tempted to say yes.

Hank laughed and rubbed his stomach. "I'll give it a good try, but if I don't watch what I eat, I'll be exercising along with Joe and Mimi at the gym."

My laughter joined his. "Yeah, right. Not going to happen any time soon." I pointed at his flat stomach.

"By the way, thanks for having your dad take Eli, Landon, and Mitzy over to see Amelia this morning. She and the boys were thrilled to be with each other. In fact, since my mom is back to take care of my sister, they're going to stay home. Even though the boys and Mitzy are a handful, Amelia couldn't stand being apart from them. Believe me, after raising seven kids practically on her own, Mom can handle those two ruffians and a small dog until their dad gets back to the States."

"Yeah, I know. My dad phoned my mom about the change in plans, but I was getting used to a houseful of energy. I'll miss them. By the way, were you questioning Tony Plum?" I asked.

"Yes, I was. Why do you ask? Is your curiosity getting the best of you?" Hank broke off a piece of the roll and bit into it.

"I ran into him on the way to your office. He didn't appear very happy with you. Were you following up on the information I gave you about Tony being upset with Mr. Sayers saying crude things to his daughters at the mall?"

CHAPTER THIRTY-THREE

Hank lowered the cinnamon bun back onto the paper bag. His crystal-blue eyes bore into mine. "Sam, you know I can't discuss an ongoing investigation. Is this what this bun is about, a bribe?" He placed the goodie back into the bag and slid it across the desk towards me.

He must have noticed the hurt look that flitted across my face since he rose from his chair, rounded the desk, and stood before me. He took my hands in his. "I know you're trying to do all you can to clear your dad's and Mr. Feinstein's name in your neighbor's murder. Believe me, so am I. It's a miracle that the chief hasn't taken me off the case because of a conflict of interests."

I pulled my hands from his and sat up straighter. My heart started to pound in my chest. "He can't. He wouldn't," I stammered. A tear trickled out of the corner of my eye.

Hank pushed off the edge of his desk and gathered me into his arms and stroked my hair. "He knows we are a couple, so I'm sure if he was going to, he would have done so by now."

I hiccupped then glanced up at him. "Really? You're not just saying that?"

"Really," he said, brushing away the tear that slid down my cheek.

"Good. Now sit down and finish the cinnamon bun. I have a bit of information for you." I flicked my hand towards his chair.

He laughed and shook his head as he walked back around his desk. "What am I going to do with you?"

I scrubbed my face free of tears and plastered on a cheeky smile. "Just love me."

He returned my smile with a cheeky grin of his own. "Oh, I do. Believe me, I do. So, what is this information you have for me?"

"Remember, you asked if I'd ever heard of a Laurine Bateman?"

Hank nodded. "Yes, and you said you didn't."

"Well, I do, or at least I did when I was younger."

One of his well-shaped, dark-brown eyebrows rose at my statement. "Well, do you, or don't you?"

I laughed. "Now *you're* impatient to learn what *I* know."

"All right, all right. Yes, I am." Hank took a bite of the pastry.

"This morning, Mom and I, plus your aunt Gladys and Candie, all had breakfast at Sweetie Pie's. That's why you're the lucky recipient of that cinnamon bun." I pointed at his sweet treat. "Anyway, Laurine happened to be having breakfast with her parents there, too. I didn't recognize her, but my mom did. Apparently, she went to private schools then away to college. She married a wealthy businessman with the last name Bateman, but Mom said they're divorced now."

Hank opened the top drawer of his desk and pulled out a notepad and pen. While I talked, he jotted down the information I gave him. "You didn't recognize her?"

"No, Mrs. Connors rarely let her daughter socialize with the landfill employees. Their families weren't good enough for her princess. I only met her a few times at company functions. You know, a barbeque or some such happening."

"Did she happen to say why she was in town?" Hank asked, tapping the end of his pen on the pad of paper.

"I got the impression she was here to see her father. He appeared in pretty poor health."

"Yeah, he didn't look well when I stopped by his house to ask a few questions." Hank wiped his sticky fingers on a paper napkin I'd shoved into the bag before leaving Sweetie Pie's. "Umm this is great but dangerous."

I sent him a questioning look. "Dangerous?"

He nodded. "Yeah, like I said, I could get hooked on these, and that wouldn't be good for my waistline."

My phone pinged in my coat pocket. I slid it out and read the message. "Mom. I think she's getting antsy waiting for me."

"Where is she?"

"I left her in the parking lot calling Marge Feinstein." I sat up straighter on the metal chair. "In fact, Mom was going to call Mrs. Feinstein and see if she and her husband were free to go out for pizza tonight. She says they are, and since I won't have the boys sleeping over anymore, that means I'm free. Care to join a lonely woman at her place? You know I'm a whiz at throwing a frozen pizza into the oven."

Hank laughed. "Are you inviting me over to bribe me with frozen pizza and have your way with me?"

I snapped my fingers then wiggled my eyebrows at him. "Curses. Foiled again. You have guessed my true motive. Any chances of me spending the evening snuggled up on the sofa with you?"

He took another bite of the cinnamon bun then swiped at his lips with the napkin. "I think there is a very good chance of that happening. I can take a break from this case for one night."

"Wonderful." I stood and grabbed my purse off the floor. "Okay, see you this evening, about six? That's when Mom says she's meeting up with her friends."

Hank joined me on my side of his desk and drew me into his arms. "Sounds perfect. That will give me time to go home and see to Nina."

"Bring her along. Porkchop would love to see her," I said, running my fingers down the lapels of his sports jacket.

He slid a finger under my chin, tilted up my head, and placed a sizzling kiss on my lips. "Remember that until tonight, but I'd better get to work if I'm going to have the free time tonight I spoke about."

I inhaled a deep shaky breath. "Okay, Porkchop and I will be expecting you and Nina about six. I'll miss you until then."

Hank walked me to his office door and opened it for me. "Until tonight," he whispered as I walked away from him.

I glanced over my shoulder and watched as he shut his door.

On the way out of the station, I waved goodbye to Wanda, who was chatting on the phone. She smiled and waved back.

* * *

"So, what did Hank have to say?"

I had barely slid into the Bug when my mom started to quiz me.

"He really liked the cinnamon bun and is coming over tonight for pizza while you're out enjoying the same with the Feinstein's."

Mom clapped her gloved hands. "Oh, goodie. I was feeling a little bit guilty leaving you home alone tonight."

I reached over and clasped her hands. "Oh, never feel that way. Lonely nights come with his job when he's involved in a murder investigation."

"Loving a police officer isn't for the faint of heart, is it?"

"No, Mom, it isn't, but he's worth it," I said as I placed the key in the ignition and turned on the car.

"Well, you two make the perfect couple. I can't wait until you tie the knot," Mom said while clicking her seat belt.

I jerked up in my seat. My foot slammed on the brake pedal. I hoped I hadn't given my mom a case of whiplash.

"Mom, we're nowhere near that stage in our relationship." In spite of the cold temperatures outside the car, sweat trickled down between my shoulder blades. What was it about the mention of marriage that sent me into a state of panic?

Mom swiveled in her seat towards me. "I never heard of such nonsense. You two make a perfect couple. Anyone can see that."

"Mom, things are a bit more complicated than us being the 'perfect couple.' This isn't one of Candie's romance novels we're talking about. First of all, I'm ten years older than Hank. Second, my marriage track record isn't the best. I'm divorced. Lastly, I wonder if by being with me, I'm denying him the joys of fatherhood."

"I've never heard of such poppycock. Of course you're not living in one of your cousin's steamy novels. No one could keep up with all of that panting and breast heaving. What does you being divorced have to do with anything? Half of the married couples out there have been divorced at some time. It doesn't mean that when you fall off the horse, you don't get right back on."

I had to smile. My mom was a treasure. She certainly had a unique way of explaining a situation.

"And what's this foolishness about denying Hank the joys of fatherhood? Has he ever said he wants to be a father? It seems to me he's quite happy being the doting uncle of quite a large crew." Mom snapped her mouth shut then shifted around in her seat and folded her hands on her lap.

I got the impression she had said all she was going to on the matter.

CHAPTER THIRTY-FOUR

—————

I chose to ignore Mom's comments and instead asked, "Do you mind if we stop at the liquor store on the way home so I can pick up a six-pack of Trail's Head for Hank to have with his pizza tonight?"

Mom settled in her seat. "No, no, please do. That sounds like a great idea. I think I might buy a bottle of wine to go with the pizza we're having with the Feinsteins."

It was a short drive to Moe's Liquor Outlet. Thankfully, Mom had no further comments about Hank and me getting married. But it niggled at me as to why the subject caused me to go into a state of panic. I knew that I loved him, so why would even the thought of spending the rest of my life with the man I adored cause me to practically go into a catatonic state?

"Oh, looky who's here. Isn't that Laurine Bateman's car?"

Mom's comment drew me back to the present. Sure enough, parked in front of the liquor store sat a silver Jaquar. The only person I knew who owned such a high-end car in Wings Falls was Laurine. "I'm guessing you're right. She must be shopping for some holiday spirits like us."

I glanced around the jammed parking lot. Laurine, Mom, and I weren't the only ones with the idea of shopping for some liquid refreshment. I snagged my purse off the back seat of the Bug. "Ready to tackle the crowd?" I asked.

"Oh, yes. I love the hustle and bustle of the Christmas season."

I smiled. That was my mom. Always up for a shopping adventure.

The din of voices hit us as I pushed open the door to Moe's. The aisles were lined with people pushing shopping carts filled with bottles of hard liquor, wine, and beer. Mom and I said hello to those we knew and headed towards the sections labeled for beer and wine.

"There… I think this Reisling will go great with a sausage and pepperoni pizza. Don't you?" Mom asked, pointing to the bottle of wine.

"It's on sale for $9.99. It will be perfect," I said as she placed the bargain bottle of wine in our cart. Connoisseurs of fine wine, my family was not. Out of a box was fine with me as long as it tasted good. "Okay, let me pick up a six-pack of beer, and then we can be on our way."

I snaked our shopping cart through the aisles towards the beer section of Moe's and placed a six-pack in the cart. "Need anything else?" I asked my mom, who was busy texting on her phone.

"Nope, I'm ready to check out. I was messaging your father. He says he's going to need a nap before we go out tonight. The boys wore him out."

I laughed. "They are a bundle of energy, that's for sure." I got in line to check out with our beer and wine. There were at least four people ahead of us.

"Oh, goodie. Look at what your dad just typed." Mom turned her phone towards me.

"What?" I asked, craning my neck towards her phone.

A smile spread across Mom's face. "He says that Amelia's husband is flying in tonight. Isn't that fabulous? He'll be home for Christmas and for sure for the delivery of the baby."

"I wonder if Hank will need to drive to the airport to pick him up." I felt a wee bit deflated thinking that would cut into our time alone tonight. Okay, so I was being selfish.

Mom shook her head. "No, your dad said her husband is getting an Uber to drive him home from the airport."

I did a mental prayer of thanks that we still had our night together.

"What do you mean my credit card is denied? I have a bigger line of credit than half the people in this hick town. Wait a minute. This one should work," an angry voice spoke from the front of the line.

My eyes were drawn, as were everyone else's, to the owner of the loud voice. I leaned around the person in front of me and saw that it belonged to Laurine Bateman. She was shoving a credit card at the cashier. The clerk pointed to where she should insert the card.

She did as instructed, but once again this card must have been denied, as the clerk shook his head at her.

"Fine, keep your cheap wine. It probably tastes like rotgut, anyway." With that, Laurine slammed the bottle of wine she was attempting to purchase on the counter and stomped out of Moe's. A Chanel scarf wrapped around her neck trailed after her as she pushed through the door.

*   *   *

I leaned into my Bug and placed the Trail's Head and my red Fendi purse in the back seat then slid behind the wheel. Mom was settled in the front seat with her bottle of wine for tonight's pizza feast with the Feinsteins.

"That certainly was an interesting visit to Moe's. Laurine sure wasn't a happy camper when she left the store, minus her bottle of wine."

I thought about my love of designer purses and the equally high-end clothes that Laurine wore. My budget was limited to designer purses that I scored on sale or online. To be able to wear what Laurine did far surpassed what I could afford. "Mom, why do you suppose Laurine's credit card was denied at Moe's? I mean, it's not as if she was trying to purchase a six-thousand-dollar bottle of Cabernet Sauvignon from the California Ghost Horse Vineyard."

Mom's mouth dropped open. "Six thousand dollars?"

"That's nothing in the wine world. Wines can shoot up into the tens of thousands of dollars," I said, putting the Bug into reverse.

"My, you are a font of knowledge," Mom said, twisting toward me in her seat.

I laughed. "Yep, that's me. Full of useless knowledge. But I'm still stumped as to why Laurine's credit cards were denied if she had married such a well-heeled man and her parents' landfill was so successful."

"Maybe she didn't make out well in the divorce settlement? Or what if Theo had some damaging evidence against her father and the landfill? That would certainly affect any income coming into the family. Theo didn't have the highest standards when it came to hurting people."

We were stopped at a red light. From my mom's last statement and the tone of her voice, it sounded as if she had firsthand knowledge of what she said.

I glanced over at her and noticed the stubborn set of her jaw. "Mom, there was more to your disagreement with Mr. Sayers than an unrequited romance, wasn't there?"

Tears trickled down her smooth cheeks. I turned on my blinker and pulled into the parking lot of the Shop and Save. I drove to the far corner of the lot most people avoided, except on Black Friday when all spaces were at a premium, as it was a distance from the store. I switched off the Bug, unbuckled my seat belt, and then turned and pulled my mother into my arms. "Do you want to talk about it?" I asked, rubbing her back in a circular motion.

She nodded against my shoulder and hiccupped. "You'd think after all these years, it wouldn't bother me. After all, I was sixteen at the time. Gosh, it was sixty years ago. I have a wonderful husband and daughter and life has gone on, in spite of what Theo tried to do to me."

My eyes flew open and my arms stiffened around my mom. What had Mr. Sayers tried to do to my mom?

CHAPTER THIRTY-FIVE

_____

I leaned back in my seat so I could see my mother better. Her perky new blonde hairstyle hung about her tear-stained face. I brushed a strand of hair behind her ear. "Mom, you don't have to tell me what happened all those years ago if it is too painful." Although, if Mr. Sayers wasn't already dead, Joe Peters would finally get his wish and have to arrest me for murder for all the pain Mr. Sayers had inflicted on my mom.

Mom let out a dry chuckle. "No, maybe if I finally talk about it, I'll be able to put it behind me. You know Theo had a crush on me."

I nodded. That had never been kept a secret.

"So did your dad. I thought it was really something to have two good-looking and popular boys wanting to date me. Your dad, though, was the one who stole my heart, but I had agreed to go to the homecoming dance with Theo."

"Was Dad too late in asking you?" I asked.

Mom nodded and laughed. The look on her face told me she was remembering my dad as a young fellow courting her. "Believe it or not, your father was shy back then, at least around me."

"Yeah, it is a hard one to believe," I said, remembering the guy wearing shorts and a Hawaiian print shirt Hank and I had picked up at the airport a few days ago.

"Well, Theo asked me first, and like most teens, I was happy to get an invitation to the biggest school dance of the year. Your memaw had already made a dress for me for the dance. I can still remember it. It was pink satin covered with lace. I felt like a princess in the dress. I even had spike high heeled shoes dyed to match."

I felt a pang of disappointment for my dad. "So, what did Dad do when he found out you were going to the dance with someone else?"

Mom smiled. "Oh, he acted his typical self. He shrugged it off and asked my best friend, Lanabeth Sullivan, to the dance."

"You didn't mind?"

"Maybe a little bit, but the excitement of going to the homecoming dance soon pushed it out of my mind."

I could remember how excited I was as a teen going to the year's most popular dance. Geez, life was so simple then. No divorce, no murders, only finding the right dress to wear. "So, what happened at the dance?"

Mom twisted her fingers together. "Theo tried to rape me."

I jerked back in my seat. My eyes widened. "What?"

"Yes, I told him I had to go to the ladies room. A ceiling light was burned out, so the hallway was dark. When I came out of the ladies' room, Theo was waiting for me. He grabbed me and pulled me into a janitor's closet, where he started to force kisses on me." Mom rubbed a hand across her lips as if remembering those bruising kisses.

"He didn't? Did he?" I asked, my hands trembling as much as my mom's.

"No. I started to scream, and luckily your dad was walking past the room at the time. He heard me and ripped open the door. Next thing I knew, he was landing some pretty good punches on Theo. In fact, I had to pull him off for fear he'd kill Theo."

A chill ran through me. Did my dad kill Mr. Sayers in retaliation for what happened to my mom all those years ago? I shook my head. No, no way. Why would he wait sixty years to exact revenge? No, my dad would have settled the matter way back then and not waited. "Did you press charges against Mr. Sayers for assaulting you?"

"No, I wanted it all to go away. I was too embarrassed and didn't want anyone to know what had happened." Mom shook her head as if trying to dispel those memories.

"How did Mr. Sayers explain away a bruised face?"

Mom laughed. "He said he slipped and fell."

"But how have you managed to live next to him all these years after what he did?"

"You know how stubborn your dad is."

I nodded. "Stubborn is his middle name."

A smile spread across Mom's face. "You've got that right. Anyway… We'd already been living here for about five years when he and his wife bought the house next door. Your dad wasn't about to let Theo force us out of the home we loved, and I agreed with him."

I leaned over and gave Mom a hug. She let out a shuddery breath. "Come on. Let's get home and put this wine and beer on ice. I have to doll myself up for your dad." She sat back in her seat and eyed me up and down. "You might want to do a little sprucing up for Hank, too."

I laughed and swatted at her arm. "Mom, he loves me the way I am."

"It doesn't hurt to give romance a little nudge," Mom said.

I turned the key in the ignition and pointed the Bug towards home. I thought over what she had said. Nope, giving Cupid a little push certainly wouldn't hurt, and I knew the outfit that would do the trick. I'd picked up a hot pink silky top and deep red velvet skinny pants earlier in the month at the Clothes Horse. I'd been saving it for Valentine's Day but thought tonight would be the perfect occasion to wear them.

* * *

"Come on, Porkchop. Hank will be here shortly. Let's go outside for a short walk so we can be settled when he and Nina get here."

Mom and Dad had left for their dinner date with the Feinsteins half an hour ago. I was showered and primped for my evening with Hank. My new outfit fit me perfectly, and I was certain he'd appreciate it. Instead of leaving Porkie out in the backyard to do his business, I felt like a bit if fresh air, too. I needed to walk off some of the excited energy coursing through my body. I donned a jacket and slipped a red and green–striped sweater over Porkchop's head then clipped on his leash. We headed down my sidewalk. The sun had set, so I carried a small flashlight with me to light my way. I was looking forward to the evenings when it would be lighter when we went for our walks.

As we walked past the Sayers's house, I couldn't help but notice how trampled the snow was from the police and EMTs from Saturday night. My flashlight caught the glow of something metal imbedded in the snow. "Porkchop, what's that?" I led him onto the Sayers's front lawn. He sniffed at the snow and started to whine. He clawed at the bright object with his front paws. Had the police dropped something during their investigation of Mr. Sayers's murder? I bent to see what Porkchop was so intent on digging up. It appeared to be the fob off a key chain. As I stared at it, my eyes widened. The logo was for not just any car, but one that stood out in small-town Wings Falls.

"I'll take that."

I whipped around to see who was behind me demanding the fob. "Laurine?"

She reached out to grab it from my hand. "That's right. It's mine."

"You killed Mr. Sayers's? Why?" I shook my head in disbelief.

"The old fool. He wouldn't listen to me when I pleaded with him to kill the story he wanted to print about my dad's landfill. I even offered him a cut of the money Dad was getting from the construction company. But would he accept my offer? Nooo, he gave me some song and dance about journalistic ethics and all that. Come on. Give it to me."

She lunged for my hand, but I was quick enough to close my fingers around the key fob. Porkchop sprang at her and clamped his teeth onto her coat.

Laurine shook her foot at Porkie trying to dislodge him, but he was holding on with all his tiny might. "Get him off me. He's going to rip my coat. It's a Burberry original. Do you know how much I had to pay for it? Probably not. You hicks wouldn't know a designer original from a Shop and Save bargain."

The next thing I knew, she was slipping her scarf around my neck and pulling it tighter. A crazy thought ran through my mind as I felt her pull the scarf tighter. Was this the designer Chanel scarf she was wearing at Moe's? If I was going to die, at least the murder weapon would be high end. I dug at the scarf with my fingers, but the sound of Porkchop's growling was growing fainter to my ears. I felt my legs begin to give way. I started to slowly sink to the snow-covered ground.

"Stop. Wings Falls Police. Stop!"

The last thing I remember was the sound of footsteps pounding towards me.

CHAPTER THIRTY-SIX

My eyes slowly opened. My cheeks were being showered with doggie kisses. Red lights flashed outside the windows. I looked around and saw I was inside an ambulance with Porkchop on the gurney next to my head, kissing me. We were traveling at a high rate of speed.

"You're conscious. How do you feel?" An EMT leaned over to observe me.

"Fine," I could barely croak out. I felt my throat. What had happened to my throat? A puzzled look crossed my face.

"Sam, you'll be okay. Laurine Bateman tried to strangle you. You're going to the hospital for a checkup," Hank said.

I glanced down to see Hank's strong hand holding mine. With my free hand, I reached up and pulled Porkchop closer to me. I tried to push up on my elbow but flopped back on the gurney. "Hank, what happened? I mean, I know Laurine tried to strangle me to get the key chain fob. She said she killed Mr. Sayers, but why? Why is she involved in all of this?" In spite of my sore throat, I had questions that needed answers.

"Money" was Hank's one-word answer.

My forehead furrowed. "Money? But she was married to a very rich man. By the looks of the clothes she wore, she was rolling in it."

"Apparently, she divorced that fellow because his business went broke and she didn't get a dime in the divorce settlement. His assets all had liens on them from banks and creditors." Hank reached up and brushed back hair that had fallen over my eyes.

I turned my head towards Porkchop, who lay with his head on my shoulder. "How did he get to ride in the ambulance?"

The EMT chuckled. "It was either bring him or risk losing my fingers. He's quite a guard dog."

"Once I took Ms. Bateman into custody, he wouldn't let anyone near you. Not even me, and I thought I was his buddy," Hank said, running a hand along Porkchop's back.

"I really am fine. Once we get to the hospital, they can give me a quick once-over, and then we can go home. What's happening to Laurine?" I said.

"I left her in the capable hands of Mimi Greensleeves and Joe Peters. They should have her at the station and are processing her for Theo Sayers's murder."

"All because of greed." I rolled my head back and forth on the gurney's pillow.

"It appears so. Mr. Connors had been blackmailing the owner of the Ferguson Construction Company for years. That's how the Connors were able to send their daughter to the fancy private school and outfit her in all those designer clothes."

"Yeah, she didn't have to look for bargains on eBay like I do," I grumbled.

"Maybe not, but think of the thrill you get when you score one," Hank said.

That was true. Porkchop stirred beside me. "What are we going to do with Porkie at the hospital? I doubt they'll let him stay with me in the emergency room."

"I already texted Candie, and she's going to meet us at the hospital. She's bringing Annie with her to coax Porkchop to leave you and go with her."

"Smart move. If Annie is with her, he'll think it's a real treat."

"Thank heavens you and Nina arrived at my house when you did. By the way, where is she?" I said.

"An officer who arrived on the scene ran her home to my house. Aaron was there to take care of her. And yes, it was fortunate I arrived when I did. When I got out of my car, I saw you struggling with Laurine and couldn't get to you fast enough. I thought my heart was going to burst out of my chest."

I felt the ambulance slow, then come to a stop, so I guessed we'd arrived at the hospital.

The EMT flung open the back doors of the ambulance.

Waiting for me was my cousin. "Sugar, are you all right? Tell me what happened. Hank said to bring Annie. She's waiting in the car." Worry filled her voice.

"Ma'am, I need to get my patient inside," the EMT said as he prepared to unload me from the ambulance.

Hank climbed down from the ambulance with Porkchop cradled in his arms. I heard him filling Candie in on all the evening's events.

Candie gasped. "Why that no-good, egg-sucking possum."

I laughed and then groaned as my hand flew to my sore throat.

"Ready for a ride?" the EMT asked as he lowered me out of the ambulance.

I nodded. Anything to get this check-up over and back home.

As the EMT rolled me past Candie, she leaned over and kissed my forehead. "Annie and I will see Porkchop home."

I reached up and squeezed her hand. "Thank you," I rasped out.

* * *

"See, I told you I was fine. Just a little sore throat is all," I said, shrugging my arms back into the down coat Hank held out for me.

"Sorry, but I wasn't going to take any chances the woman had hurt you."

I turned and snuggled into his arms. "Let's get home and have that pizza feast I promised you. Although I might stick to ice cream until my throat feels better. I'll text Candie and tell her all is well with me and that we'll be home soon."

Officer Reed had delivered Hank's Jeep to the hospital. I had refused the customary wheelchair ride to his car and was released into his care.

As I reached in my coat pocket for my phone, I heard Hank's ping from his jacket. He pulled it out, and a broad smile crossed his face. "I think we'll make a small detour before we leave the hospital."

Hank took my hand and led me to the elevators at the end of the hall. "Where are we going?" I asked, curious as to why we weren't leaving the hospital and heading home.

"You'll see in a few minutes. We weren't the only ones busy this evening." Hank punched the elevator button, and the stainless-steel doors slid open. "After you, madam." With a flourish of his hand, he motioned for me to enter the elevator and pushed the button for the second floor. He stared at the elevator's metal ceiling and started to whistle.

"You're not going to tell me where we're going, are you?" I asked, a puzzled look on my face.

He glanced down at me and shook his head.

I heaved a sigh and resigned myself to letting him keep his secret. Within seconds, the elevator stopped and the doors slid open again, arriving at the floor I least expected, the maternity floor. It suddenly dawned on me why we were here. Amelia.

"She's having her baby?" I gasped out. Excitement filled me.

"Had," Hank said. He took my hand and led me out of the elevator and down the tiled hall towards the nurses' station.

The walls on this floor were embellished with scenes from nursery rhymes. Humpty Dumpty sitting on his wall and children holding hands and skipping in a circle were only two of the many happy images decorating the walls.

"But Amelia's husband just got home, right?" I asked, trying to keep up with Hank's long strides.

"Yes, he'd no more dumped his gear at home then had to rush Amelia to the hospital."

We arrived at the nurses' station. A friendly young nurse whose name badge said she was Ms. Pace looked up from the computer she was studying. "Can I help you?"

"Yes. My sister, Amelia White. I believe she was admitted a couple of hours ago."

"Ahh, yes. She delivered her baby about an hour ago. She's not quite up to receiving visitors yet, but you can go to the waiting room around the corner and wait for her husband if you like?" Ms. Pace pointed down the hall.

"Thank you, we'll do that. I'll text her husband, Matt, and let him know we're here."

Nurse Pace smiled and nodded. "Congratulations on becoming an uncle. The baby is beautiful."

Hank thanked her, and we headed in the direction of the visitors' waiting room.

"She didn't say what your sister had," I said.

"No and that's going to be a surprise."

We made the short trip to the waiting room. The room was outfitted in cheerful colors with yellow painted walls and pink and blue plastic molded chairs. A mobile of white horses with orange polka dots hung from the ceiling. We were the only ones in the room.

"I'm going to let Matt know we're here," Hank said, pulling his phone out of his coat pocket.

Hank chuckled and smiled when he got a reply from his text.

"What's put the big grin on your handsome face?" I asked, running my hand down his stubble-roughened cheek.

He turned his lips into the palm of my hand and kissed it, sending a thrill through my body. "You'll see in a few minutes when Matt gets here."

CHAPTER THIRTY-SEVEN

———

We didn't have long to wait for Matt. A handsome soldier dressed in his Army greens bounded into the room moments later. He looked to be in his early thirties, and he had the same red hair as his son, Landon. Father and son were mirror images of each other.

Hank pulled him into a big man-hug. When they stepped apart, Hank slapped him on the back and said, "Congratulations, man. How's Amelia doing?"

"Great. Just great. She got her wish with this baby, a girl. Not that we wouldn't have been fine with another boy, just so the kid was healthy." He turned to me. "We didn't want to know what the sex of the baby was going to be ahead of time. Wanted it to be a surprise, but had our fingers crossed for a girl."

I was caught up in Matt's good mood. Excitement ran through me at the thought of a new healthy baby.

"Matt, this is Sam. I'm sure Amelia's told you all about the two of us," Hank said, pulling me next to him.

Matt reached out his hand to me. "You bet she has. Sorry we haven't met before this, but I've been busy serving Uncle Sam."

I shook his hand and said, "Congratulations on the new member of your family, and thank you for your service." It was a big deal to me to thank members of the service and veterans for serving our country.

"Thank you, ma' am. I appreciate it."

"Sam. Please call me Sam," I said. Even though I'd just met him, I really liked Matt. He was friendly and had an engaging smile.

"The baby and Amelia are fine, right?" Hank asked.

"Better than fine. Amelia's a bit tired. Her pregnancy has been rough the last couple of weeks, but it's over now and the baby is healthy. I was sorry I wasn't here for her," Matt said.

Hank cuffed Matt on the shoulder. "Amelia understood. Your life isn't your own when you're in the service."

Matt nodded then dug his phone out of his pants. "Here, let me show you some pictures of the new member of the White family." He scrolled through his phone then turned it towards Hank and me.

The picture showed a tiny person swaddled in a pink blanket, cradled in Amelia's arms. The baby had a tuft of red hair and was sucking on her thumb. Amelia was staring down at the little bundle, her eyes filled with motherly love.

"Do you have a name for her?" I asked.

"Yep. We thought since she was born at Christmas time, she's Noel," Matt said.

"Oh, that is sweet. She really is a bundle of Christmas joy."

Hank nudged Matt's arm. "Go ahead, tell Sam what her middle name is."

Matt cleared his throat. "Well, Amelia and I were thinking, if it's all right with you, we'd love to have her middle name be Samantha, after you."

My mouth fell open, and tears filled my eyes. They had named their daughter after me. I looked up at a smiling Hank. "You knew about this?"

Hank nodded. "I confess, I did. I knew you wouldn't mind."

"Mind? I'm thrilled," I said, giving Matt a hug.

"Umm, that's not all. Amelia and I have one more request."

"Sure, what is it?" I couldn't imagine being more tickled than having a baby named after me.

"Would you consent to being her godmother?"

My knees became weak as I sagged against Hank. "Godmother. I couldn't be more honored." A smile spread across my face, and I rubbed my hands together. "Oh, let me get my hands on Noel Samantha. She'll be the most spoiled baby in all of Wings Falls. Wait until she gets older and I take her shopping."

Hank laughed. "Uh-oh, Matt. You and Amelia may want to reconsider your choice of godmother for your baby girl."

I playfully swatted Hank's arm. "No, you don't. You know I'll love her to pieces."

Hank hugged me to his side. "Yeah, I know you will. We'd better let Matt get back to Amelia and take you home."

Hank shook Matt's hand, and I gave him a hug and told him to give Amelia our best and a kiss for baby Noel from me.

* * *

On our ride home from the hospital, Candie had texted to say she was heading out since my parents were there. She said she didn't mention the night's events to them. She thought she'd leave it up to me to tell them whatever I wanted to. Porkchop jumped at our feet when we walked through the door, yipping and wagging his tail. I scooped him up in my arms and hugged him to me. Mom and Dad were dressed in their fuzzy pajamas and about to head off to bed. They'd had a few glasses of wine too many and were ready to sleep them off. Hank and I filled them in on the night's events before they retired for the night. I downplayed what had happened between Laurine and me so as not to worry them too much. At their age, they didn't need to know all the gritty details.

I gave them both a kiss and wished them a good night's sleep.

"Would you like me to pop a pizza into the oven?" I asked. It had been a long and eventful evening.

Hank ran a weary hand through his wavy hair. "No. But a Trail's Head would be fine."

"Okay, I'll be right back." I turned towards the kitchen with Porkchop trotting beside me, I was sure in anticipation of a treat.

"I'll give the station a call and see what's happening with Laurine," Hank said, pulling his phone out of his quilted vest.

When I returned to the living room with his beer and a basket of pretzels, he had ended his conversation.

"What's happening with Laurine? Is she being booked for the murder of Mr. Sayers?" I asked, handing him the beer and placing the pretzels on the trunk in front of the sofa. I sat next to him and curled my legs up under me.

"Thanks," Hank said, taking the bottle from me. "She's got a lawyer and was read her rights. But she has been charged with Mr. Sayers's murder and the attempted murder of you."

My eyes widened. "I hadn't thought of that. But I guess she did try to murder me, too. And all for what—money to buy some fancy designer clothes and accessories."

"It was fortunate that I arrived when I did. When I got out of my car, I saw you struggling with Laurine and couldn't get to you fast enough. I thought my heart was going to burst out of my chest."

"So, it looks like Rosa didn't kill her husband and really does have a new love interest. I wish her happiness. She certainly deserves it after all those years living with her nasty husband," I said, snuggling closer to Hank.

"Yes, I checked the fellow and her out. Apparently, they met in high school. She's been able to email him on the sly without Theo knowing. As for Laurine, greed has been the cause of a good many murders. But enough talk of murder. Since your parents have gone to bed and left us a bit of privacy, would you care to take advantage of the mistletoe?" Hank asked.

"I thought you'd never ask." My heart warmed at his smile.

Hank took my hand and led me over to the archway between the dining room and living room where mistletoe hung. I stood poised for a kiss, but instead he got down on one knee. He reached into the inside pocket of his vest and pulled out a blue velvet covered box. My whole body started to tremble as he flipped open the box's lid. Resting inside on a bed of satin, the most beautiful solitaire diamond winked at me rivaling the lights on the Christmas tree.

Hank looked up at me with love-filled eyes. "Sam, will you do me the honor of becoming my wife?"

My hands flew to my mouth. My brain screamed *Nooooo*, while my heart shouted *Yeeeees*.

What would my answer be?

The heck with listening to my brain. I was crazy in love with this wonderful man. I knelt down in front of him and held out my left hand. "I want to spend the rest of my life with you."

Hank's eyes filled up. "So, the answer is yes?"

I nodded, my own eyes tearing up at the emotion he was showing. "Absolutely," I said as he slipped the ring on my finger.

ABOUT THE AUTHOR

Syrl Ann Kazlo, a retired teacher, lives in upstate New York with her husband and two very lively dachshunds. Kibbles and Death is the first book in her Samantha Davies Mystery series, featuring Samantha Davies and her lovable dachshund, Porkchop. When not writing Syrl is busy hooking—rug hooking that is—reading, and enjoying her family. She is a member of Sisters in Crime and the Mavens of Mayhem.

Learn more about S.A. Kazlo at:
www.sakazlo.com

THE SAMANTHA DAVIES MYSTERIES
Kibbles and Death
A Doggone Death
A Wedding Gone to the Dogs
Pups, Pumpkins, and Murder
Chilled to the Dog Bone
Mistletoe, Mutts, and Murder

Made in United States
Cleveland, OH
24 November 2024

10861004R00106